Cover design by: Carly Hall

D1737154

ISBN: 9798507314225

To Mom and Dad, for always teaching and training me in the Lord. Also thank you for teaching me to be a respectable man.

Acknowledgments

There are many people I am grateful to for helping me with this book. First of all, one of my friends gave me the concept cover. It looks so good, and I am thankful to him for all his work. He truly put lots of time into it and wouldn't take anything in return.

Carly, thank you for the countless hours of work you put into creating the final cover design. Without your standout cover my book would not be as good as it is now. I thank you for the willingness to take time out of your life to do this and your attentiveness to deadlines.

Kimberly, Jessica, Jazmine, Olivia, April, William, Gracie, Jill, Jayden, Ruthanne, Annastasia, Aaron, Julie and countless others, thank you for the reading, thoughts and impressions. Without your reviews and feedback, some major plot points that would have never changed. I couldn't have done it without you all. The advice you all gave was different. Some in a quick conversation while others were long talks in hammocks. So many of you desired and truly wanted to see this book succeed and I thank you for all the work you have done to help it get there.

Mom, Dad and the rest of my family thank you for giving me the time to work on my book, even when it seemed like I was spending too much time on the it. I thank you for getting on me about spending more time on editing when I should have been doing school. Thank you also for letting me

6

take short breaks from school to work. You were all so supportive as I racked my brain for plot points and story changes.

Characters

Slaves on and off Plantation

Hasani Davis, *Middle-Aged Male, African*

Jamilia Nelson, *Middle-Aged Female, African*

Hashim Jones, *Middle-Aged Male, African*

Kamau Davis, *Middle-Aged Male, African*

Sarah Wilson, *Older Female, African*

Fred Williams, *Middle-Aged Male, African*

Tiana Nelson, *Middle-Aged Female, African*

Solomon Nelson, *Older Male, African*

Logan Miller, *Middle-Aged Male, African*

Slave Owners/Overseers

Jonathan Hundley, *Older Male, American*

Jon Hundley II, *Middle-Aged Male, American*

Adam Hartless, *Young Male, American*

Judah Matthewson, *Middle-Aged Male, American*

William Turner, *Middle-Aged Male, American*

Underground Railroad Conductors

Reverend Johnson, *Older Male, American*

Aaron Schrock, *Older Male, Amish*

Caroline Schrock, *Older Female, Amish*

Anna Walker, *Older Female, American*

Present Day Family

Charlette Thompson, *Teenage Female, American*

Chandler Thompson, *Teenage Male, American*

Charlie Thompson, *Teenage Male, American*

Kim Thompson, *Middle-Aged Female, American*

Eddie Thompson, *Middle-Aged Male, American*

Grandpa Thompson, *Older Male, American*

Introduction

The Love of a Slave began its writing during the pandemic/riots of 2020.

I have wanted to write this storyline for a long time. The story follows two friends as they learn what it is like to trust, to love, and to forgive. I hope to show in this story that even when it is hard to trust God, we need to believe He is in control, and will take care of us. This book is fiction, but it is based on real facts and true stories. I hope that you enjoy it!

This book wasn't just a book to get on the market or a book to just finish but the lessons written here are lessons I have learned through my years. I hope that you will enjoy what I have written in this book and my prayer is you will learn something just like I did.

I hope to portray in this book how we are to treat people around us, whomever they may be. We shouldn't let what race or ethnicity they are determine how we act around our fellow humans. No race should be treated with more partiality than others. In God's word in James 2:1 "My brothers and sisters, do not show partiality as you hold on to the faith in our glorious Lord Jesus Christ."

Almost 50% of the world is female. The way some men treat women in this day and age is despicable. We as men, need to be chivalrous and treat all women with respect and honor. They are very important and deserve to be treated better than they are.

Men have gone soft and views have changed. But we as men need to stand up and make a difference in the life of women.

I hope this book will make you think a bit about our world and how it was. Many things are different and some aspects were harder than what we are going through in the present and beyond.

14

Reviews

Definitely worth reading! This book will make you smile, cry, and get really attached to the characters. It has many levels of mystery and suspense that makes you not want to ever put the book down. I highly recommend reading it!

April Smith - Camp Ministry Coworker/Close Friend

I admire Noah's mission to create stories that honor God in both message and morale. The lessons within this book are ones that our culture needs.

Carly Hall - Cover Design Illustrator

An excellent read, Noah has developed into quite the author. The character development in this book will leave you feeling like you're there, immersed within the story. This story was well thought out and researched to be appropriate according to the time period, giving many details and insights into the conditions the people had to go through. Noah's delivery of the gospel intertwined into his characters will leave you contemplating Christ's love for all of us! Thank you for tackling such a topic especially in today's culture.

Aaron Keller - Editor of <u>The Love of a Slave</u>

You become highly invested in the characters of this story, to the point where they are no longer characters but people. As you follow their journey you can't help but sit up straight and bite your lip as you watch them struggle toward freedom. Highly recommend this read. Educational, well written and passionate.

Gracie Heider - Author of <u>The Guardian Angels</u>

Very well done! When I thought I got the story down a plot twist came up! It definitely keeps you on your toes as you read each page. You will feel suspense, anger, joy, and fear along with the importance of the message of the story. It's eye-opening and a highly recommended read. Proud and excited for you Noah, great job.

Annastasia Hinman - Chapter Title Designer/Lifelong Friend

I was blown away by how this book put me through all the emotions and taught me a little more about the lives of those in slavery and those who helped them. Thank you, Noah, for bringing history back, by way of these characters, and

reminding us power that Christ's love &
forgiveness can have on our life.

Jessica Soares - Middle School Teacher/Close Friend

Table of Contents

The Love of a Slave

1 The Harsh Beginning

On the morning of April 20, 2020, Charlie, Chandler and Charlotte Thompson woke up to their mom calling them to breakfast. They all dragged themselves out of bed and slumped downstairs to the kitchen. There on the table waiting for them were some hot pancakes and their mom Kim, and Dad, Eddie, sitting in their chairs, ready to eat. They all took their seats and prayed over the food. As Eddie was praying, Chandler bowed his head and unlocked his phone. The three kids all had a serious problem with their devices. The three couldn't even last ten minutes without checking something on their phones. It was a big problem and Kim knew it. Like a good mother should, she looked up during prayer to make sure the kids all had their heads bowed and were praying. But what she saw shocked her! All three were looking down at their phones; the very phones she had bought for them! She certainly did not buy them so that they could use them during prayer. As she bowed her head, she knew that she had to put an end to this. So, she decided to have a talk with all three that night.

Eddie finished the prayer and Chandler quickly put his phone away as his mom said, "Grandpa will be coming today so, I want the house clean before he gets here."

The triplets all replied, "Yes Mom" and ate their pancakes.

After breakfast Chandler, Charlie and Charlotte left the table to clean the room they shared. But once they got to their room, they all sat on their beds and opened their phones.

Chandler and Charlie had a bunk bed on the right of the room, while Charlotte had her own bed on the left. Their room was not very big, but it was big enough for their beds and a desk for homework. After about fifteen minutes their mom walked in and was shocked yet again. All three kids jumped off their beds and stuffed their phones in their pockets. But they were too late. Kim had caught them and she put out her hand and said, "No phones today. You should have been cleaning. Now get to work." As they finished cleaning, the doorbell rang. They heard their mom open the door and greet someone. It had to be Grandpa since he had planned to stop by. Grandpa was the most uncultured person they knew. He did not use a cell phone, nor did he use any new technology for that matter. The most recent technology that he had was a TV set from the 1970s.

She invited him to have some pancakes that were still warm. Just as Grandpa sat down, Eddie walked into the room dressed in his police officer uniform. Before leaving for work he called to the kids, "Alright time to come down and hang out with Grandpa." He kissed his wife and headed to his cop car to go to work.

When Grandpa had finished eating, he got up from the table and went into the living room where Charlie, Charlotte and Chandler were all on their tablets. Grandpa had never understood the appealing new technology. He sighed and sat down on a couch across from his three grandchildren. As he did, Mom came into the room. "No devices while I am gone. I am going to run some errands. And we will be having a talk about your device use tonight." All three put their tablets on the coffee table in front of them.

Right when Mom left Grandpa said, "Okay, so what shall we do? Could I tell you a story?"

Chandler sarcastically replied, "I can also read a story on Instagram." Charlie and Charlotte both laughed, but Grandpa didn't.

"Ok, you can read us a story, but what is Instagram? Is it a book you have? I've never heard of it."

Annoyed, Chandler sighed and responded, "Never mind, it was just a joke."

Grandpa said, "Okay, I am going to tell you a story. But you have to get comfortable. This could take a while. It all began back in 1863, in Monroeville, Alabama."

--.--

It was a warm, humid Monday morning. Hasani Davis had slept all of the previous day. Most of the other slaves went to their black

church on Sunday but Hasani didn't. He wished
he could go home. Sunday was the only day
Hasani did not work. There was no use wasting
time thinking about the past. Hasani got dressed
and headed out to work. It was 4 o'clock in the
morning, so the sun would be coming up in an
hour, and it was just light enough to see. This
was the usual time Hasani woke up. He lived in
a room they called the slave house. The house
was just one big room that had dozens of cots
lining the walls. There was a sink in the corner
and a fireplace on the left. It was small but just
big enough for all of the slaves. Master Hundley
was always bringing in new slaves and it was
getting tight. Hasani was nineteen years old. He
was a slave living on a large plantation in
Alabama. With his muscular build he had been
sold for a good price, five years earlier. He
didn't like to think about the past, about how he
had been sold into slavery. But those thoughts

forced their way into his mind, and he began to replay that terrible time, so long ago.

Hasani had grown up in the woods with his father, mother, and brother, Kamau. His parents told him they had been transported from Africa when they were teenagers. His father had fallen in love with his mother on the ship to Virginia. They were sent to Ohio, on a truck, once they got off the ship. They managed to get off the truck that was taking them to Ohio and make their way to Indiana which was a free state.

***

One day, when Hasani was eight years old, he went to the market with his father to buy food. They lived in Indiana where slavery was outlawed so they lived safety and freedom in town. Everything seemed perfect in Hasani's life, until that day.

On the way to town, he talked with his father. His father said, "Your name is Hasani. You were named after your grandfather. And he died trying to save me from being sold into slavery. When I was thrown on the ship, he attacked the men. But the men had guns and killed your grandfather. Never let your name be anything but Hasani. You have a good, strong body. Whatever you do, stay in Indiana. If you ever leave, you will be in danger. The danger is called slavery. That means you will be forced to work for white men, and they will not pay you. I work for a white man, but he pays me money to buy food. We are free black people; nobody is able to sell us into slavery." Just as he said that four men ran up and grabbed Hasani's father. Hasani began to fight the men, but they threw the boy back into a pile of baskets and quilts. They tied up his father and put metal things around his hands. The men threw him in a cart, and rode off, before Hasani could stop them. It was so hard for Hasani to see his father taken away. He ran home as fast as he could with tears streaming down his face. When he got home, he told his mother, who burst into tears and ran to town. Once she got there, she ran to the sheriff's office. The sheriff told her that they would try to find her husband. They looked for over two weeks and only found out that the men were able to capture Hasani's father and take him out of state to sell him into slavery where it was legal.

It was so hard for his mother after the loss of her husband. From time to time, she refused to eat. She tried to move on, but she never truly got over the trauma. She was so heart-broken by her husband's disappearance; she began to get sick. She spent much of her time inside the house with no fresh air. She began to fade over the years, her health worsening. It was left to Hasani and Kamau to care for her.

One day Hasani asked his brother to go with him to get some berries for dinner. Kamau always loved picking berries because he was able to eat all he wanted and still have plenty for dinner.

As they walked out to the berry patch they began to talk. Kamau said, "I checked on mother before we left, and she is not going to see many more days. Her birthday is next week so we need to plan something big. This could be her last birthday with us." Suddenly, they heard a gunshot back at the house. Their hearts dropped and they looked at each other with fear-stricken faces. They turned around and ran as fast as they could back to their cabin. When they got there, a few men saw them and grabbed the boys before they ran away. The bigger man, who had a long mustache and a fuzzy shaved beard, put gunny sacks over their heads and put them in a wagon. After a long and very bumpy ride, the boys were lifted from the wagon. Kamau attempted to attack the men, but they were too strong to be overcome alone. With tears streaming down his face, Hasani asked, "What did you do to mother and what will you do to us?"

The man looked over at Hasani and said, "Your mother was not strong, but you seem strong enough, son. I could get a good price for you. From now on your new name will be James and your brother's name is Daniel." When Hasani heard that, the tears came faster, and his anger brewed remembering what his father had said before he disappeared. The pain was too much to take in so he ran at the man and began to punch him. Hasani may have been only fourteen, but he was strong. He knocked the man over, but three others were able to tie up Kamau and Hasani. Once tied, the men forced them up onto a platform in front of a group of people. There was a man in the crowd at the auction named Jonathan Hundley. He saw the two boys and he paid top dollar for them.

Jonathan Hundley put both boys in the back of his buggy and said, "It's a very long way, so get comfortable. You are gonna be back there for a long time." Hasani and Kamau lay there tied up, but with Hasani's strength and flexibility he was able to squeeze out of the ropes tied around his wrists. He shuffled over to Kamau and began to untie his ropes. But the buggy hit a rock that was on the roadway and Hasani lost his balance falling from the back of the buggy. Jonathon was out of the buggy before Hasani could even blink. When he made eye contact with Jonathon he stood up and ran off. He wanted to help his brother, but he would have no chance at escaping, so he fled on his own. Jonathan yelled for him to come back but it was no use.

Hasani didn't stop running until he got to the center of town. For once, the muscular tall Hasani felt so small and scared. Although he was free for now, he was no longer in a free state, so he had to watch his back. He looked around and finding nothing to do, with no money, he walked into the closest saloon.

As he walked in, he was instantly bombarded by the unfamiliar scent of whiskey and other alcoholic drinks. He scanned the room and saw there were upper hotel rooms and a lower section which was where everyone was drinking. In the corner was a man playing a piano and a few people were around listening to music. There were multiple tables around the room filled with men and women. There was a game of poker going on at the table near him and there was a bartender serving drinks to the men at the counter. Hasani walked over to the counter and sat next to an older black man and a saw a drunk, unconscious man slumped over the counter. He also got a few confused stares from some of the men and women. Hasani called for the bartender who had been eyeing him since he came in, "Can you get me a whiskey?"

"For whom?" the bartender replied.

"Me, of course," Hasani scoffed.

"You are only a boy, how old are you?" the bartender questioned.

"I am 18, now get me a whiskey" he lied.

The bartender looked at him and said, "You got any money?"

"Uhhh, yeah course I do," he snapped.

"Let's see it then!" the bartender said doubtfully.

Hasani looked down and saw some cash in the hands of the drunk man who was now leaning on him. He snatched the money and slammed it on the counter. The bartender took the cash and filled a shot glass of Jim Bean and placed the bottle on the counter next to Hasani. Hasani lifted the glass to his lips and tasted the ice-cold taste of whiskey. It was sharp and it slid down his throat so easily. He couldn't resist filling his cup to the brim one more time, then another, then another and soon the bottle was empty. Hasani was drunk.

Hasani yelled for the bartender to bring him another, but the bartender would not give this boy one more drink. Hasani looked into the bartenders' eyes and said, "Get me a drink now or I will smack the taste out ya mouth." The bartender glared at the drunk boy with a look of disgust. Hasani didn't hesitate and grabbed the bottle and smashed it over his head, knocking him to the ground. Everyone went silent and watched the furious, but injured bartender slowly stands while blood trickled down the side of his face.

A man in the back of the room then yelled, "Don't let the boy leave!" Everyone then ran at him, fists clenched ready to fight. Hasani attempted to defend himself which started a fight between everyone. Some people were so drunk they didn't know who to attack so they just punched the person who was next to them. In the heat of the fight, a young white man stepped inside. He was wearing a black ten-gallon hat, a black leather vest that covered a white blouse, and at his hips were two Colt Paterson revolvers, along with a belt loaded with .36 caliber bullets. With each step on wooden planks of the saloon, his black cowhide leather boots with rowelled spurs, pounded a toughness that commanded the room. As he walked through the swinging doors, he removed each revolver and shot a bullet through roof. Dust and debris fell and the room went silent.

The stranger spit into a metal can. He looked around and said, "What's going on here?" He looked and saw a bartender with a kitchen knife about to stab Hasani. "Give me the boy or you will have a hole in your head so big I could see through." The bartender dropped the knife and let the boy go. The mysterious man grabbed the boy around the shoulders and walked him outside the saloon. Outside, two horses were waiting. One was a big, muscular brown horse, and the other was a black horse, a bit smaller and not as strong. The man said, "My name is Jon. Please climb onto the black horse. It kinda looks like you." he chuckled. Hasani didn't laugh and was offended that he was compared to a horse but climbed on anyway. Jon motioned for him to follow, and they rode out of town.

Hasani and Jon talked a lot on the ride. They talked about where Hasani had come from, and Jon had talked about his childhood. According to Jon, he had been born in a monastery. He grew up in church until he rebelled and left his religious past to be a cowboy and to rescue those who needed saving. Now that he had done that it was just up to him to uphold what he planned to do with the rest of his life. Hasani and Jon became close friends. Hasani never really knew where they were going but he didn't want to ask because right now he was safe.

After many days of travel Jon said, "We are approaching our destination."

"This is a great place, is this your home?" Hasani asked.

"Yes, this is my home," he said as he dismounted his horse. Hasani also dismounted and walked towards the house. Jon followed behind and called for his father.

His father came through the door and said "Welcome!" Hasani looked and saw so much familiarity in his face.

Behind him he heard someone say, "Hasani, is that you?" He knew instantly who that was. The distinct voice of Kamau lingered in his ears. He turned and saw Kamau running to him. Noticing it was Kamau things started spinning in his head. He heard the click of a gun and felt Jon's gun pressed into his back. His heart sank. He had been betrayed by Jon, the man who he trusted and had saved his life. He lost all his trust in men that day and could never trust anyone ever again.

***

And that was how Hasani had ended up here, five years later. Hasani and Kamau had vowed they would never go by their new names, because these were not their true names. The first two years had been extremely hard for the boys. It had been tough growing up working every day. They were not used to such work, but as they got older, they became accustomed to the slave life.

Each morning, as Hasani dressed, he woke up the older teenagers. The rule stood that if you were up late you would get whipped, and your workload would be doubled. Their master, Jonathan Hundley, was a mean man. He did not care about most of his slaves. He only cared about the ones who made his food, like Sarah Wilson. Sarah was the head cook in Master Hundley's kitchen. She had worked in the gardens until last year's harvest.

***

On a Monday afternoon during the harvest season, the slaves were taking a break. Master Hundley was looking for a good cook. Sarah had been working in the fields all day. Because she was a woman, she was allowed to stop work early. She came back to the house and prepared stew for all working slaves. The men got off work at 5:00pm each day and came in to eat. Hasani was last in line, so he got a little extra soup. He thanked Sarah for the stew and went to sit by the master's house. The sun was still out but there was shade there, by the house. As Hasani sat down, Master Hundley walked around the side of the house. When he saw that one of his slaves was eating a full bowl of stew, he decided he needed to try some. So, he said, "You there, James is it? Give me your stew. If you don't, I will make you wish you did."

Hasani had no choice, so he reluctantly gave up his meal and said, "Here, and my name isn't James. It's Hasani!"

Master Hundley shrugged it off and tried the stew then said, "Wow, this is very good. Tell me now, who made it?"

"Sarah Wilson made it. She makes food every night. Please don't make her stop."

Master Hundley just sneered and walked to the slave house. After about two minutes Master Hundley came out holding Sarah by the arm and walking her to the house. Since then, Sarah had never returned to the slave house.

***

This morning was very dry. Hasani could tell it was going to be very hot today. Once everyone was up, they all headed out to the fields. They had to be as quiet as they could because if they woke up the master they would be in trouble. There were guards who stayed up all night. They were on a rotation to make sure all the slaves never escaped. Jonathan Hundley owned exactly thirty-six slaves. Hasani knew most of them personally. The only slaves he didn't know too well were those that worked in the house. Hasani's best friend was Hashim Jones, a tall, strong boy two years older than himself. Hashim had also vowed not to go by his slave's name. The slave catchers had named him David, but he wouldn't have it. He had attacked the man who named him and almost killed him. But then three other men came and were able to hold him down. Since he had been so aggressive, he was whipped. It was the worst whipping he had ever experienced.

As Hasani, Hashim and the other slaves headed to the field, they heard the head slave catcher say, "I am going today with the master to go bring back three more slaves. So, y'all better be ready for them when we return." Hasani wasn't too surprised. Master Hundley was getting new slaves all the time. So, he just saw this as another way to make a friend. His master rarely brought back girls, but Hasani overheard that he was trying to get a few today. He had never made a close friend that was a girl. Maybe this would be the time.

2. The Plantation

While working in the field, Kamau told Hasani he was leaving for good. Hasani was shocked; Kamau was very brave, but to try to flee was beyond bravery. This was certain death. Not many slaves got out free. Hasani did everything possible to talk his brother out of it. But all Kamau could say was, "My mind is made up. I'm going in two weeks, no question. You need to come with me. There is a man who is going to nail me into a wood box and ship me to Indiana. Indiana is a free state." Hasani did not believe that running away was the best thing to do. He knew that if he didn't escape, he would be stuck here at the farm. But there would be a risk of death if he tried to sneak out. Kamau began to tell him of all the things that he could do when he was free. But Hasani's heart was hardened, and he would not agree to bolt to freedom.

In the early evening they got off work and headed back to the slave house. It was sad to arrive with no good stew waiting. There was only stale bread and food that had been thrown out of the master's house. Hasani gathered what food he could and went to eat with his best friend, Hashim. Just as they sat down, the master, returned with new slaves. He had been gone all day purchasing men and women to increase his power and wealth. Everyone came out of the slave house to see who Master Hundley had purchased. As Hasani and Hashim walked to the back of the wagon one of the overseers took a girl about eighteen or nineteen by the arm and pushed her out of the wagon. She fell out and hit the ground with her knees. The girl cried out in pain as she fell. This man had no care for how he treated the slaves and continued pushing them out of the wagon. Hasani hurried over to the girl who was pushed out first and helped her up. The girl thanked him for his kindness and asked if she could have some water. Hashim had a canteen, so he gave her what was left. Then he asked, "What is your name? My name is Hasani, and this is Hashim."

The girl responded, "My name is Jamilia Nelson. Thank you for the water."

Hashim just looked at her, repeatedly asking if she was ok. Jamilia tried to stand but her legs were badly bruised. It appeared the slave catchers had beaten her. This made Hasani angry because he hated the way some people mistreated blacks, especially women. So Hasani picked her up and carried her to the slave house and laid her in his bed.

The next day Hasani woke up and was surprised that he was sleeping on the floor. He stood up and looked at his bed, suddenly remembering why. Beautiful Jamilia Nelson was there, sleeping soundly. Hasani quietly bent over and gently woke her. She calmly opened her eyes and looked at Hasani, seeing the care and concern in his face. He said, "We have to go to the field now so get ready. I'll show you what to do today." Jamilia accepted his invitation and began to get out of bed, but the bruises on her legs were too painful. As she collapsed to the floor, Hasani reached down, put her arm around his neck and helped her back onto the bed. He told Hashim what the problem was and both decided it was best to leave her in bed for the day.

On the way to the fields Hashim said to Hasani, "I have wanted to talk with you for a while. These slave catchers are brutal to us, and you know that. They do not treat women any better than men. I know you have seen this."

"Yeah, I have seen it and it disgusts me," Hasani said.

"Whatever happens, we must protect the women in our life. They should be treated with compassion," Hashim said, "We must honor the women and possibly even sacrifice ourselves for them. The slave owners just treat them like dogs. They beat them, whip them, and do terrible things to them just for fun. But men should not be like that. We need to care for the women even if we have never seen them before."

Hasani then added, "Yes everything you are saying is true, but it is so much easier said than done. I would say that I would, but who knows. If the situation came up, would we really be brave enough to be able to stand up for them?"

On the way to the field, they stopped at the work shack and get their job assignments because it was the start of a new month. Hashim and Hasani were both assigned to weeding and tilling a new garden on the east side of the farm. The work shack was on the west side, so it was a long walk to get to the garden. They also had to walk by the central barn. The central barn was one of the worst buildings on the plantation. There never was anything good going on there. They use it for the buggy and for punishing slaves in private. Hashim and Hasani both looked at the barn as they walked past hating every square inch. The most disgraceful things happened there, torturing, punishing and even putting slaves to death. That's not even saying some of the additional terrible things they did to women.

When they got to the barn, they saw a slave catcher was whipping a young woman, just as

Hashim had warned Hasani before. Seeing this instantly made Hashim enraged. Hasani tried to calm him down, to tell him not to fight but instead to take her place. But Hashim did not hear him, Hasani turned to implore Hashim to stop, but he was too late. Hashim was gone and running at the man. Gripping the man by his shirt, he pulled him in front of his face and threw a hard punch on his right jaw, knocking the man onto his back. Hashim was so angry he straddled the man and continued his attack. Hasani called out to his fellow slaves to assist pulling Hashim off the man. As they removed the enraged slave, the man lay there with a bruised and bloodied face.

Hasani yelled at his friend, "What were you thinking? You can't just attack people like that! Yes, I saw what he was doing, and it is not right. Beating him up is not the best idea, you could have taken her place."

Hashim looked at Hasani and said, "Do I even know you? Did you not pay attention to what I was just saying? I thought you were agreeing with me, but I guess I was wrong. Let's just get to work."

Hasani yelled at him as he walked away. "Now you are going to get whipped really bad if not something worse. This is your fault. I have no part."

With that, they headed to the field and began to work. During their work, the slaves liked to sing. The song "Go Down Moses," which was written about the Israelite slaves in Egypt, was a favorite among these slaves. The Israelites were slaves to a man named Pharoah, who had a heart of stone. Hasani had only heard it from others who said it was in Exodus, the second book of the Bible. Pharoah needed his slaves and wouldn't allow Moses to lead them out of slavery.

Being such a good friend, it was hard for Hashim to hold a grudge, so he came over and worked next to his friend. He said, "Sorry for getting so mad at you. You are my favorite person in life, and I couldn't bear to go into the torture that I expect, being mad at you. Will you find it in your heart to forgive me for getting so angry at you?"

Hasani looked at him and said, "Are you serious? Of course, I will forgive you. I care about you so much. You are my only friend in the world, and I am so thankful you are saying sorry, because I am sorry as well."

"In the future, a better option is to ask to take the woman's place or try to talk to the slave hand. Don't just be so quick to attack a man.

You understand? Hashim nodded and returned to his work.

At mid-day, Hashim was called to the master's house.   He knew what was coming to him. He had prepared for this moment hoping he would be able to endure the pain. As he slowly made his way to the house, Hashim was met by Master Hundley's son. His son had been gone doing out of state work for the past few years. Now he was twenty-one years old and had come back to help his father and was put in charge of the slaves. This would make it so that Master Hundley wouldn't have to keep track of the slaves.

Master Hundley was an evil man, but he was nothing compared to his son. When Hasani was first brought to the farm he had been betrayed by Jon whom he had trusted. Everyone had heard that Jon Hundley loved putting pain on slaves.

Jon showed Hashim no mercy. The slaves could hear the crack of the whip from the fields. The whipping and torture lasted hours.

3 Heartbreak

The sun poured down a blistering heat. While in the field working, the sun seemed so much hotter, especially when there wasn't much water. There were also rules that must be followed, while in the fields. The slaves were allowed one break at noon. You weren't allowed to go back to the slave house till the work day was over. If an overseer saw something they didn't like, they had free reign to whip. If you didn't bring your own water, then you made a big mistake. If you passed out due to heat exhaustion, other slaves would lay you in a shaded area and you would be left until you woke up. Once you woke up, the overseer would make you get back to work. Hasani had only passed out a handful of times in the five years he had been there.

Late in the day, at about 4:00pm, just an hour before they got off work, Hashim showed up. The day had been long, just like every other day. But today seemed even longer because Hashim wasn't there to keep Hasani company. When Hashim arrived, his shirt was ripped, and his back had been shredded by the whip. The blood was dry now, so the wounds would crack every time he moved his back. He told Hasani in almost no voice, "I'm working all night with no other slaves. Please pray for me."

"I will pray for you and if you need me to stay out here with you, I can."

Hashim was a God-fearing man, but Hasani was not. Hasani just could not understand how a God who loved him would let him go through such torture. Even though he said he would pray, he knew he only said that to make Hashim feel better.

The two friends worked through that last hour but, then Hasani was forced to return to the slave house for the night. When Hasani returned he saw Jamilia waiting for him. He forgot about Hashim and ran to her.

As he reached her, he said, "Wait, you are standing, do your legs not hurt anymore?"

"They are still hurting," she said, "but I can walk now."

All of a sudden Hasani was grabbed by the shoulder and spun around. He turned and looked into the fiery eyes of Master Hundley's son, Jon Hundley. "I saw YOU in the fields. But where was this girl you're talking to? I didn't see her. You know that everyone is required to be working, no matter what. I am guessing she is with you, and I don't want to see that again! Now girl, come with me! You'll be working the whole night." Jon snapped.

Jon took her by the arm and pulled her out to the field. Hasani watched as he took her away, "WAIT, I WILL TAKE HER PLACE!" Hasani shouted.

"I told her that SHE is working, not you. You will be working double tomorrow, so get a good night's sleep. I expect you in the fields before dawn," he snapped.

Hasani was shocked, "But sir, that's so early, and it's when the wolves come out."

Jon was getting angrier, "I gave you an order. Are you going to do what I say or do you want double all week?" He paused for a second and pointed his finger at Hasani and said, "If you try to run away, you will be caught. You have no

way of escaping. We just got twelve
bloodhounds yesterday to make sure NOBODY
escapes," he growled. Hasani dropped his head
and walked back to the slave house.

That night, Hasani did not sleep. He
stayed up all night watching the figures in the
field. It might have been night, but it was still
75° in the middle of July. Maybe the Master did
not care about them, but Hasani did. When he
was dressed and had water for Jamilia and
Hashim, Hasani walked out to the field to work.
As he reached the field, he saw that Hashim had
passed out and was pale. He had lost too much
blood; He was in so much pain already, that the
all-night work was just too hard for him. The
overseers were stern and very cruel. They would
not help anyone even if they needed water. The
man who was overseeing the night workers
looked strong and fast. So Hasani pushed away
the idea of getting away. He ran over and gave

Hashim all his water. This was all too much for Hashim. He could not work after such a whipping. So Hasani leaned his friend against the tree to rest. Although he was unconscious, he made him as comfortable as he could. Jamilia had already filled many baskets with corn and looked like she was exhausted. Hasani walked over to her and told her to lay down and rest. So Hasani let her sleep for an hour.

They were in a five-acre patch of corn so she could lay down anywhere and not be spotted. It would take so long for it to be fully harvested. While she slept, Hasani got to work gathering corn.

As each minute passed, he felt like someone, or something, was watching him. He knew that the overnight slave watcher was watching him. But he felt that something else was out there too. He had a really weird feeling that Hashim was in danger. But he just shook off the thought. He looked around and spied several figures running through the corn. He saw one near a big rock on the far side of the field. The figure then climbed onto the rock, threw its head back and let out with a blood-curdling howl. Hasani knew at once, what it was. It was a lead wolf summoning his pack.

Hasani's hair stood on end. He looked over at Jamilia, who was sleeping soundly. Hasani was shocked that she hadn't been awakened by the howling. But he had the feeling again about Hashim, so he ran over. When he got there, he found the pack had beaten him. The slave watcher was just watching with his rifle pointed at them. He was watching the wolves the whole time but didn't say anything. Hasani ran over and began yelling and throwing rocks at the wolves who all turned to face him. He frantically looked around for a weapon. He instantly found a large staff, picked it up and began batting away the wolves. They fought back viciously biting and clawing, but Hasani was able to overpower them and chase them away.

Once they were gone, Hasani ran back to his friend, who lay on the ground, blooded, with his right arm torn badly. Hashim was still alive but fading quickly. Hashim looked at Hasani with weary eyes, and said quietly, "Hasani, take care of Jamilia." Tears streamed down Hasani's face. Hashim had been his best friend ever since he was brought to the plantation. Hashim had defended Hasani all the time and Hasani had defended Hashim. Hasani remembered the days when they were young and had easy work. When they just had to move rocks and clean the yard. So many years of laughter and fun. Hasani could barely contain himself.

The night watcher just watched them and was grieved in his heart. He saw, for the first time, how much these slaves had feelings. He knew they did not deserve to be treated this way. He decided to go to the master and quit the next day.

Hasani pulled Hashim into a hug and held him as he lay there suffering. Hashim opened his hand and a small piece of paper fluttered to the ground. Hasani picked it up and unfolded it carefully.

Hashim said, "I wrote this for you but never gave it to you." Through tears, Hasani read it out loud:

August 10, 1858

Once I met the best friend anyone could meet. You are not like other people. You are fun, and you are a true gentleman. I pray that one day you will see and believe in the one true God. He is the God who came to die for us, to make us truly free. Not free as in free from slavery, but free from guaranteed death. God is like the Good Master. We are His servants, but He loves all His slaves. We need to accept him as our Master to enter into his kingdom. I love you Hasani, and I hope to see you in Paradise. Always remember that you were the most important person in my life.

As he finished reading, his tears flowed unchecked. Hasani screamed out, "GOD PLEASE DON'T DO THIS! JUST DON'T LET HASHIM DIE!" As he said this, Hashim slipped away from this earth. Hasani closed Hashim's eyes and said, "GOD WHY? I WILL NEVER FOLLOW YOU! YOU HAVE TAKEN EVERYTHING FROM ME!"

Hasani stood up, left Hashim's body and walked over to Jamilia. She had watched it all. He hugged her and the tears fell again. In his heart, he cursed God and said, "I will never ever follow you. You say you saved him from death, but Hashim just died, so that's on you, God. You took my mom, dad and now my best friend. I will never trust you." Jamilia then took him back out to the field to continue their work.

Jon watched all this happen from the porch. Hasani hadn't realized that Jon was there, but Jon sat back with an evil grin. After looking away from Hasani, Jon saw something about Hashim that Hasani didn't notice. Jon stood up and walked over to the night watcher. "You may take the night off. I know what trauma that may have been for you." The night watcher thanked him and went inside. Jon walked over and put his fingers on Hashim's neck. Confirming what he thought, he laughed. He knew that if the body was gone when Hashim returned, it would make it worse for him. So, he slumped Hashim over his horse and rode away. After about twenty minutes of riding, he reached a river, where he dumped the lifeless body into the cool water. Hashim's body rolled quietly into the depths of the river. Jon rode home contented at the thought of making Hasani's life more miserable.

4 Escape

One week had passed since Hashim had died. Hasani was surprised at how fast Hashim's body had disappeared. Hasani was a wreck. It was so hard to lose a best friend. Jamilia did everything she could to comfort him, but nothing worked. Then, on Saturday, something happened.

It was the middle of the day, and the sun was at its hottest, making work harder for everyone. Their clothes were drenched with sweat. Hasani was doing everything he could to just get through the day, knowing he could rest on Sunday. As he worked, the reflection of something blinded him. He looked around him swiftly and spotted it.

Something metal was in the same place Hashim had died. So Hasani ran over and just as he reached for it, a large boot stomped down. Hasani looked up into the fiery eyes of Jon Hundley. Jon smirked and bent down to pick up the object. He stood up; they both saw that it was a golden pocket watch. Jon saw it and his eyes went wide. He quickly popped it open, and a slip of paper fell out. Jon picked up the paper and read it quietly. Hasani caught a glimpse of it. *"You need to go to church to learn about God. -Hashim."*

Jon, not realizing Hasani had already read it, ripped it up in front of Hasani's face. "What a nice pocket watch. I think I'll keep it for myself. Oh yeah and condolences for your friend," Jon

cackled. Hasani then turned around to head out
to the field.

As he was walking, he thought. *Even
though Hashim told me to, I cannot go and
worship the God who took everything from me.*
So, he joined Jamilia in the field. She had been
so supportive ever since she had arrived. When
he reached where she was, she said, "I saw what
happened and I am sorry you couldn't keep it.
But truly the watch wouldn't have made you
happy for long. The way you can have forever
happiness is the way you treat people. But not
only treating people good but also trusting in the
God who saved us. The way you take leadership
and value people for who they are not for their
skin color or for their money."

Hasani listened to everything she said.
Hasani admired her for the wisdom that she
displayed. But he responded saying, "Trust in

the God who saved us?! Are you serious? If God is willing to save us, then why did Hashim die? That doesn't seem like a loving, saving and forgiving God. I could never follow your God. I like you but I don't agree with your religion." With that Hasani walked away to get to work. Jamilia was heartbroken, but knew that she couldn't give up on him. She had to keep loving him and showing God's love through her actions.

That night as Hasani walked back to the slave house Jamilia ran to catch up with him.

Jamilia wanted to lift his spirits, so she said, "I am going to stay up late tonight to look at the stars. Do you want to stay up with me?"

Hasani couldn't turn down that offer so he said, "Yes, I will! We could climb up the slave house and watch the stars up there. It will be a better view from there."

That night Hasani and Jamilia snuck out of the slave house with plans to stargaze. They quietly opened the door hoping not to wake anyone. They had to walk slowly around the slave house to get to the ladder. When they got around one side, they saw a night watcher manning his post. If he saw them, they would be accused of escaping, and they could lose their life. But they were able to quietly get to the ladder and onto the roof. They found a place at the roof to sit down.

The sky was very clear that night. As they watched the stars something happened inside of Hasani. He felt like he genuinely loved this woman. He gazed at her and remembered all the things he had gone through with her. He had just met her a few months ago, but she had supported him when he lost a friend and she cared for him. Hasani got lost staring at her.

Jamilia looked over sharply and laughed saying, "I thought we came out here to stargaze? You aren't looking at the stars, you are just looking at me."

"I thought the stars would be beautiful tonight, but they are not even close to as beautiful as you." Hasani said.

He then reached his arm around her and pulled her close to him. When Jamilia felt his arm, she felt a wave of comfort from the man she loved so dearly. She looked into his eyes and saw true compassion. It was the same compassion from the day she arrived. That was when she first fell in love with him. She then laid her head down on Hasani and they watched the stars. Jamilia knew that this was the man that God had directed into her life. But she knew it would be hard knowing the difficulties of his faith.

About an hour later, Jamilia stood up and said that she wanted to show Hasani something. Hasani stood up and said, "Okay what would you like to show me?" Jamilia grabbed his hand and led him to the edge of the roof. Hasani was confused when he saw just forest for miles.

Jamilia broke the silence by saying, "Look, see how the forest goes on forever. Every few miles there is a house. The houses are all in a straight line. Well, the houses are like that all the way to Indiana. Indiana is where I am from. I used to be free. I lived free with my mother, father, and my older sister. But one day when my sister and I were playing in the woods, we were kidnapped. We were thrown into a wagon and brought here to Alabama where we were sold into slavery. My sister was taken somewhere else to which I do not know, and I was taken here. I just assume that my father was also sold into slavery and my mother was murdered. My mother was sick, and no slave owners wanted to take sick people. I want to escape from this slavery. I want to be free! That row of houses is a route of homes that are safe. They are all people who want to help slaves get to freedom. They have places to hide in their houses and they have food and new clothes. It is called the Underground Railroad. I want to escape someday, but I don't want to do it without you."

Hasani said, "I can't escape now. I want to wait and think about it for a little while." Just as he said that a cold breeze swept by. It sent a chill down Hasani's back. It also made Jamilia shiver. Hasani said, "It's getting late, let's head inside." As they were heading back to the cabin Hasani saw someone run by and out to the road. In the road, was a buggy and once the figure climbed into the buggy, it quietly went away.

Today was the day that Kamau had been waiting for. Ever since he had been brought to the slave plantation he wanted to leave. He hadn't been tortured to a point that leaving was necessary. But there was an urging feeling inside yearning for freedom. He wanted to live his own life and be his own boss. He had always had his mind on escaping, and he had even tried a few times. Now that a solid plan had come, he was ready to make his escape. Kamau quickly packed everything needed for the trip. Things like an extra pair of clothes, a knife he had stolen, some food and an old picture that was taken of him and his father. The buggy would be getting here very soon and once it arrived, he needed to leave right away, or he would get caught. Kamau got ready to go then went to say goodbye to his brother. He had tried so hard to get Hasani to come with him, but he wouldn't hear of it. Hasani was too afraid of death, and he felt like he was safe here. There hadn't been much persecution done to him yet. And Hasani was in love, so he couldn't just leave his other friends behind. But it was too late to think about that now. Kamau tiptoed over to Hasani's bed to say goodbye but was surprised to see he wasn't there. He looked all around, but was losing time to catch the buggy. So, he wiped away his one tear and ran out to where the buggy was going to be. There were three-night watchers on duty so he had to be quiet as he ran. They kept a good eye out, but having to stay up for long hours in the night they weren't as alert as they should be. He quietly walked through the bushes and saw the buggy. Kamau bolted for the buggy hoping to get to it without being seen. The plan was to climb into the back and pull a quilt over his head. But one of the guards saw the buggy leaving and gave chase. The driver of the buggy, Ethan

Herbert, saw the guard chasing after and slowed down. He told Kamau to stay still and quiet. When the guard reached the buggy Ethan asked if anything was wrong.

The guard said, "Yes, I saw a man run to this buggy. He had one bag on his side. He looked like a runaway slave."

The other man who was sitting in the passenger seat got up and said, "It was me, we both deliver letters, and I was just running to get done faster. If you want to see, there is a letter in your mailbox. Now can we continue to finish our route?"

The guard who was half awake just said, "Ok, yeah, whatever, sure keep going." Finally able to breathe, Kamau realized he had passed his first obstacle, but knew his challenges were not yet over.

5 Indiana

As Kamau relaxed his body, he contemplated his decision to leave. He might never see his brother again. He then began to think about his father and where he had been all these years. He had tried to figure out where he had been taken, but he had no real leads. That afternoon, they arrived at Ethan Herbert's home. Before he jumped down, Ethan put a jacket on Kamau so that he couldn't be seen by other people. He then helped Kamau down and rushed him in so he wouldn't be seen. There was a man who gave him a briefing on what would happen. Kamau would be mailed in a wood box to the select location and Ethan would open up the box, once he was in free territory. The trip would be several days since they were in Alabama, and he was going to Indiana.

Indiana was a free state. That meant there was a law in Indiana that outlawed slavery and anyone caught selling or forcing African Americans to work would be imprisoned. All the states in between were not free states so you had to go through dangerous territory if you wanted to get free on foot.

Once Kamau had learned all that he would need to know he climbed into the box. He got as comfortable as he could in the wood box knowing it would be a long journey. There were holes on the side of the box so he would be able to breathe. He had enough food and water to last him a few days. There wasn't enough room to carry more bags and personal items other than the clothes on his back. The men shipping him then nailed the box closed and brought it to the mail station. Kamau was excited yet scared at the same time. If anyone opened the box or found out what was inside, they might kill him. When Ethan reached the mail station, he put the address on the box, and had it loaded onto the mail wagon going straight to Indiana.

The trip was long and exhausting and very, very bumpy. After about a day's travel they hit a big pothole and the box was thrown from the back of the wagon. The man driving the mail wagon didn't see it, and continued down the trail. Kamau wanted to call out, but then the man would know what was inside. If the driver found out it would jeopardize the entire plan and his life.

After two days of sitting on the side of the road another mail buggy came down the road. Seeing the box, the two men driving stopped the wagon, got down and saw that it was a package for Indiana which was on their way and about a day and a half journey down the road.

The men picked it up by the sides to load it onto the buggy. Kamau woke up as he felt himself moving. He saw through his small box holes that it was another mail wagon and breathed a sigh of relief. The relief was quickly taken away when the men threw the box into the back which put ,Kamau upside down. Within fifteen minutes, Kamau had passed out due to too much blood rushing to his head.

Once the box had arrived at Indiana it was put on the post office porch on its side. After another full day Ethan finally had found it and claimed it. He opened the box and pulled Kamau out. Kamau was not dead, but almost. He had only gone two days without water, but longer without food. He started with enough food and water to last him the trip, but it spilt when he had fallen asleep. He also passed out for one and a half days. Ethan had helped him escape and was able to build him back to full health. Kamau had done it; he was a free man.

***

The morning light shone through the cracks in the slave house, which woke up Hasani. He realized he woke up late, so he jumped out of bed, but was surprised that not many others were awake. Last night was so romantic, but today something was happening.

As Hasani awoke from his slumber he heard Jon and his men scrambling around, saddling horses and untying the hounds. From the looks of it, Hasani knew of the slaves had escaped! Hasani's heart dropped out of his stomach as he slowly turned to look at his bed. Since he was sleeping on the ground and Jamilia was on his bed, but he was comforted when he saw the eyes of the woman he loved. Hasani's thoughts reverted back and then remembered his brother Kamau saying he would escape in a couple weeks. Hasani knew that Kamau must have been the slave that had escaped last night. He hadn't recognized Hasani in the darkness.

That day was a long one for Hasani. Every time he heard a dog bark, he thought about his brother, Kamau. He knew that if Kamau was ever found, he would be killed.

The next day Jon and all his men returned. He could tell that they did not find Kamau, and Hasani's heart soared. Hasani kept hearing Jon swear about not being ready and having his dogs on duty during the night. He had the dogs all tied up during the night.

Jon and his men got back in the later evening and went straight to the slave house. He threw open the door enraged, then scanned all the faces that were inside. Everyone immediately stopped what they were doing. Children were playing with toys on the floor and some men and women reading books throughout the house. Most slaves never learned to read, but there were some mothers who had learned as little girls. After assessing the room, Jon was unable to locate the person he was searching for.

Jon stormed to the sleeping room. He walked straight up to Hasani and looked him in the face and said, "Where is your brother?!?" He was now very angry, but Hasani couldn't answer his question. All he had seen was a figure running in the night, to a buggy.

"I will not ask again Mr. Davis, where is your brother?" Hasani tried to say he didn't know where he was. But when he opened his mouth, a fist punched him which sent him falling back onto the floor. Jon stepped over him and looked him in the eyes. "You brought this on yourself. Until you tell me where he is going you will never see the inside of this building again."

Hasani was taken out of the slave house and into the central barn. There he had his hands tied to the brick wall. Then Jon began the interrogation. With every question that took too long to answer he was either punched or slapped. Jon was not a nice man, and his evil seemed to intensify as the days grew on.

As the grueling days went on, word got around to the slaves of what had happened to Hasani. Jamilia was devastated at what was happening. Every night, Jon swore that he would let Hasani go only if Kamau was dead or if he killed him. Hasani would not yield and give in to telling where Kamau was heading. After one full week, Hasani began to fade. He had been able to survive on the water he was given once a day. But he was losing energy quickly.

He was dying from dehydration and lack of food. He was getting weaker, and was losing motivation to live. He knew that if he could see Jamilia's shining face one time he would be motivated to live on for as long as he could. Finally, after a many long days and more torture than he could deal with, Hasani gave in.

During one of Jon's many interrogations Hasani yelled out, "STOP! Will you let me free if I tell you where he is?"

Jon smirked and said, "Yes, I will make it worthwhile for you."

Hasani then told him, "Kamau was shipped to Indiana. That is all I know. I swear it."

Jon laughed a sly laugh and left the barn. Hasani yelled after him telling him to free him, but Jon didn't even hesitate. With that, Jon told his men and they all left on horse. Hasani was left in the basement to die there and Jamilia knew it. But Jon was paying other slaves to keep her secured in the slave house. There was no one who could help.

Just before Jon left, he stopped at the top of the stairs and told some of his men who were staying, some terrible news. He said, "I want Hasani dead by the time I get back. If he isn't, you will all be dead!

That night a figure snuck down the steps to the basement. The figure went as quietly as they could. Hasani heard it right away since he couldn't sleep tied to the wall. The figure walked over to Hasani and pulled out a large kitchen butchering knife. The figure then raised the knife and brought it down hard. Hasani winced, waiting for it to get over. But the knife landed in the wall near his hand. How could someone be that bad of an aim? He looked up and saw the silhouette of the figure raising another knife once again. This time it didn't hit him but near his other hand. The figure then stepped forward and picked both knives and pulled them out of the wall. Hasani fell forwards and onto his face. Struggling, he looked up and saw the figure had lit a lantern. The face had been lit up by the brightness and Hasani let out a sigh of relief seeing that it was his old friend, Sarah Wilson. She lived in the house because she was the cook. She didn't get good living conditions, but she still got a roof over her head. Since she was inside there were no guards to get past.

Sarah snuck him out of the barn, and he met Jamilia who shed tears seeing him again.

They both had to lift him most of the way to their slave house but when they got him to bed, they laid him down and gave him food. The other slaves had stopped keeping Jamilia secure because they had already been paid the money. Jon had paid them to make sure Jamilia didn't help Hasani.

The next day, Hasani and Jamilia went to the black church. Jamilia put on her nicest dress and Hasani wore his pants that had no holes yet. This was a special Sunday. It was Hasani's birthday. He was turning twenty years old. He did not care too much, so the only person who knew was Jamilia. Kamau had told her everything about his brother Hasani. Kamau had always thought that Jamilia was the best girl for Hasani.

When they arrived at the church building. They were stopped by a white man with dark brown hair. He was wearing a cowboy hat and a nice suit. He looked very rich. Hasani had no idea that he was the driver of Kamau when he had escaped. Hasani squeezed Jamilia's hand. Hasani cared for her and would do anything to protect her.

The man said, "Hasani, calm down. I may be white, but I treat blacks with the respect they deserve. I have a proposal for you. If your master finds out, you will die. Will you listen and keep it a secret?

"Yes, what is it?" Hasani asked.

"My name is Ethan Herbert. I have a message for you that is top secret. Your brother is safe, and he told me to give you this letter. Read it and let me know if you want to follow in his footsteps. But I can only help one slave every few weeks. If your wife here wants to leave, she would be a few weeks behind you, but it isn't guaranteed you will arrive at the same place."

Hasani responded by saying, "Thank you for the letter and she is not my wife... yet. I will let you know when I make up my mind." With that, Ethan walked away from Hasani and Jamilia. Hasani tore open the letter as fast as possible and read it quietly.

September 17, 1863

Dear Brother, How are you doing? I pray for you every day. I pray that you will receive Christ as your personal Savior. When I arrived in Indiana, I went to a church and my heart was softened to the words of the Lord.

You are probably wondering how I am writing this since you know I can't read or write. I am speaking while a man writes down what I say. You are also probably wondering how I escaped.

I went to a man named Ethan who offered to help free slaves. He is the man who gave this to you. He has helped many slaves in the past with a good chance at getting to freedom. I asked him how hard it was to escape, and he told me everything there was to know about the path to freedom. I thought that I would have to run for miles and miles on end to reach freedom, but I didn't. Ethan put me into a wooden box and nailed it shut. The box had holes on the side so I could breathe. It was an awfully long trip. I fell out of a buggy and then was picked up a day or so later. When I was finally picked up by another postal wagon, they took me to my destination. After a couple days, Ethan saw the box and took me to his mother's house. When he found me, I was starving and completely unconscious. He pulled me out and put me in his

feather bed. Now I am living like a regular
gentleman. I have a job at a blacksmith shop in
Fairmount, Indiana. Please come and be with
me soon. And one more thing, take good care of
Jamilia.

Your Loving Brother, Kamau

Hasani folded the letter and walked
Jamilia into the church. Hasani sang all the
songs that morning. He knew them all because
so many of the slaves either sang or hummed the
tune while working. When the pastor went to the
front Hasani bent down his head and fell fast
asleep. He didn't care for the preaching he just
liked the singing and music.

One hour later, Jamilia shook Hasani
until he woke up. "The service is over Hasani,
and you can't just sleep in church all the time. If
you listen, you might learn something from the
pastor."

Hasani said, "I know, and I am sorry, but I just do not find interest in religion. Yes, the songs are nice and I like to sing but I don't really like all the preaching." With that he stood up and put Jamilia's arm in his and began to leave the church. As he was leaving, he was stopped by a man named Fred Williams.

Fred walked up to him and said, "I am a slave that was just purchased by your master last week. I am good friends with Ethan Herbert, so I know what has happened. Also, word gets around, so I know what happened to your best friend, David, wasn't it?"

"His name is Hashim, not David, and what do you want other than to bring me back the hurtful memories?" Hasani's face saddened as he thought back.

Jamilia soothed him by saying, "Hasani calmed down. He sounds nice."

The man responded by saying, "I have a time when you can get free by taking the underground railroad. This will let you two flee together under the cover of darkness. You have a particularly good chance of surviving, but there is a chance you will die. Don't make up your mind now. Let me know if you want to take my offer."

6 The Price of Love

The day had been a long hot one. It had to be
reaching about 100° Fahrenheit. They did the
usual tasks; shucking corn and pulling weeds.
The slaves who worked in the fields always had
so much envy for those who worked in the
house. They were able to work in the cool air all
of the time. While they were nice and cool in the
house, the field workers were outside sweating
like hogs. Hasani wished that he could just have
something cold to drink. Thinking about it made
his mouth water. He had gone all day with
nothing to drink. It was so hot, and he was
wearing dark clothes. He took off his shirt, but it
didn't change much. He was still dripping with
sweat. As he looked around, he could feel

himself starting to fade. He knew if he didn't get something to drink, he would pass out. That's when he saw Sarah walking outside and about to pour out a pitcher of water. Hasani stumbled over to her tripping and falling. When he reached the porch which was only fifty feet or more, he got on his knees and said, "May I have some water?"

She said, "Yes, I will pour it into your mouth, but you have to get back out to the field before the master finds you." Right when she poured the water, a strong hand grabbed Hasani by the shoulder. As the water was about to hit his face he was yanked back, and the water spilt onto the ground. Hasani jumped up and began to drink out of the newly formed puddle. The water had landed in a dirt pile, so it was seeping into the ground quickly. Hasani then stood up face to face with Adam Hartless, one of Jon's newest overseers. (Yes, his name actually was Hartless. It perfectly described him as a person.)

Although Adam knew nothing about what Master Jon had been doing to him, he did not like Hasani. This was the first time that Hasani had seen him this mad and so uncompassionate you could say he was heartless. Before Hasani's heart could drop, a fist flew and hit the bottom of his left jaw. He blacked out and crumbled to the ground. Adam turned around and took out his beating staff.

Hasani did not come to, until that evening. He woke up laying in his bed that he had given to Jamilia. He looked around then rolled over. He wanted to see if Jamilia was laying on the ground next to him. But instantly, there was pain all over as he moved his body. As he rolled, he felt like his right arm was crumbling. After much effort, he was finally able to flip himself over. He reached down and touched Jamilia's hand. She woke up at once and looked up at him. A wave of relief went over her face once she saw that Hasani was alive. She then said, "You were knocked out by Adam. After you fell to the ground, he grabbed his staff and beat you for a long time. Your arm is broken. Other than that, you just have bumps and bruises."

Today was not Sunday but, Thanksgiving Day. Just last year, President Abraham Lincoln had proclaimed the first national holiday of Thanksgiving, to be celebrated every November. The master and his family traveled away for that weekend. They left the grounds under control by Adam Hartless. This man was not nice, but he was not as mean as Jon. Hasani stayed in the slave house for one day so that he could rest.

The next day Hasani went out to the fields. He was able to work with one arm while the other was in a sling made from his other shirt. As he worked, he watched Jamilia. She had been working so hard recently. If it weren't for him, she would have probably escaped a long time ago. But he knew that she was caught in between the two loves of a slave; love & freedom. She couldn't just leave Hasani behind and risk never seeing him again. They might kill Hasani because of their love for each other. If she left, they would think Hasani helped her escape. Hasani also knew she loved her sister so much, and wouldn't leave without her.

This made Hasani think, he didn't want to make Jamilia feel like she had to stay here forever. He planned to take her outside tonight under the stars and tell her that they would escape soon.

--.--

August 8, 2020

Grandpa said, "Alright kids I have been telling you this story for a long time. Time for a break. Let's go eat, Your mom is back, and she has made some grilled cheese sandwiches for us. We can get some lunch and finish the story afterwards."

The three kids all stood up and headed to the kitchen without touching their tablets or any devices. This was the first time they had gone so long without even thinking about a device since they were teenagers.

As they sat down at the table for lunch, they ate in silence.

After some time, Charlette said, "Grandpa, this story is better than any movie I've seen on my phone. I guess there is some value in being off the phone for a bit." Grandpa just smiled and winked at his daughter ,who then winked back.

After they finished eating, the three kids ran back to the living room. Grandpa expected them to get back on the tablets, but they didn't. All three kids were sitting on the couch waiting for him to continue his story. Grandpa eased himself into the rocking chair and said, "Ok, where were we?"

Charlie piped up and said, "Hasani was just about to tell her that they were going to escape."

7 Frantic Escape

December 13, 1865

The way back from Indiana for Jon had been a long trip; two full weeks to be exact. Jon just hurried inside and went straight to his room.

Before he walked in, Sarah stopped him by saying, "Master, just to let you know, the killing of Hasani has been carried out," she lied. Jon smiled and laid down in his bed hoping for a good night sleep. They had not found Kamau in Indiana which made him angry. He planned to have a chat with Jamilia about what had happened.

***

After a long day of work Hasani was finally able to spend some alone time with his favorite girl. it got As it got dark, they snuck out to the field without the guards seeing and laid down on the grass. Watching the stars Jamilia said, "So what did you want to tell me?" Hasani couldn't hold back his smile. He had planned this all day. Now it was time.

"So how would you like to visit houses all the way to freedom?" Jamilia sat up so fast and stared him in the eyes. Hasani could see the excitement, but also a touch of fear in her eyes.

Trying to be quiet she said, "When are we leaving?"

He chuckled and said, "Soon. I have to make a few arrangements first."

As they walked back to the slave house quietly, Hasani thought about when they should leave. He was taking a big risk for even talking about such things with a fellow slave. Hasani thoughts then turned to what would happen if they were caught. Suddenly a light was turned on in the house and Jon stepped out onto the porch. He saw the two figures in the field instantly. Even from that far away, Hasani could feel his anger. Jon didn't hesitate and picked up his whip. He then picked up a staff and ran to catch the two slaves who were on their evening chat. But to Jon it looked like an escape.

Jon's adrenaline was spiking. Jon noticed who it was almost immediately. He had been so cruel to Hasani already that it seemed logical that he would try to escape. Jon was also stunned that he wasn't dead. Before Jon had left, he had told his men to kill him. But since Hasani had been set free, Jon's men just never told him. But Jon vowed to never again let any slave escape from his father's farm. Just thinking about it being his father's farm made him mad. HE wanted to oversee the farm. HE wanted to be able to treat the slaves how he thought they should be treated. HE even had the vision of one day taking over the farm and having full control.

Hasani could feel his fear all around him. He was afraid of so many different possibilities. The chance of getting killed and that would be the end of the line for him and Jamilia. Or he could just be whipped very badly and that would set them back from escaping until he was healed enough to run. If his back was shredded from whipping, then he would not be able to run at all. Even walking could hurt depending on how bad the whipping would be. His arm was still healing so he had to carry it in a sling. It wouldn't affect his running having one arm in a sling.

Hasani braced himself for the expected confrontation with Jon. But Jon just dropped the whip. Hasani had a weird thought that Jon was going to forgive them. But then a sly smirk came across his face. This quickly wiped the thought away. Jon then turned his eyes to Jamilia, and his eyes looked her over from head to toe. Hasani's blood boiled; he was furious. He squeezed Jamilia's hand and she moved closer to him. Jon said, "I have figured out your punishment. First Hasani, I will kill you, then teach this pretty lady how to be a..." But before he could say anything Hasani punched him on his jaw. He thought he could hear the crack of his jaw breaking. The impact sent him falling to the ground and spitting out blood.

Hasani looked down at him and said, "Don't mess with her. She is no toy; she is a woman just like your mother. You should have more respect for women even if they are black."

It was clear what Jon was going to do to her and it made Hasani sick just thinking about it. Hasani was about the same size as Jon. Jon was a good three inches taller, but Hasani was much stronger. He'd had the full week to get stronger.

Hasani then picked up the whip off the ground and tied Jon up to the tree. He then ripped off his shirt and used it as a gag to keep him silent. As they were leaving Hasani spun back around to face Jon. Jamilia thought he was about to fight him, so she tried to stop him. But instead of punching him he grabbed the pocket watch Jon had taken away from him and walked away with Jamilia.

Hasani popped it open and looked at the time. It was 12:32. With all that done, he knew that had to escape that night. He would be killed if he stayed much longer. Jon could not yell loud enough and Hasani had tied a good knot. Jon wasn't getting any help till morning. He would get to morning that is, if he survived the night. But little did Hasani know was that Jon had a knife in his left hand.

Hasani and Jamilia ran back to the slave house to gather personal items. They had to leave as fast as they could and not take too much. While getting their things, a slave was awakened to the sounds they made. Now that this slave saw what was happening Hasani had to tell him what was happening. The slave that had been woken up was Fred Williams. He had been a boxer before his slave days, and had a strong man build. Fred followed Hasani asking if there was anything he could help with. He also continued to ask if he could go with. Finally, Hasani agreed to let him join in their escape. A strong man might be helpful if ever in danger.

Hasani, Jamilia and Fred collected everything they needed and headed for the door. They were already preparing for freedom where they wouldn't be slaves any longer. A smile crept across Hasani's face as he reached for the door handle. As he squeezed the knob it was turned from the other side. What Hasani saw was the silhouette of two men in the doorway. The smile left ten times faster than it came. There in the doorway was Jon and Adam, who had been awakened by Jon. Jon chuckled and said, "I thought you two had already left. This will make my job much easier." Jon then raised a loaded two barreled shotgun to Hasani's face.

Just as he was about to pull the trigger, Fred ran past Hasani and at Jon. Jon fell to the ground and Fred was instantly on top of him throwing punch after punch. Hasani could see that Fred was trying to start a fight with Jon to give them time to run. As Hasani watched the two men fight back and forth he awoke from his trance and reached out to help Fred. But then Fred was thrown back into Hasani's arms. Fred whispered urgently, "I am alright. You MUST leave without me. I can distract him for a while. GO!"

Hasani then said, "We will keep you in mind, but we will go." They didn't have to worry about Adam who was still trying to get Jon free and also get Fred off him!

Jon didn't notice Hasani fleeing but he yelled at Adam. "Go Get My Men!!!"

8 A Life for a Friend

Hasani and Jamilia began their long
escape in silence. It was night and they wanted
to be far away before they started talking.
Hasani was awfully glad that he had snatched his
pocket watch from Jon. Now he was able to
keep track of time and know when to stop. They
had to travel by night and rest by day. It was
4:00am, and the sun would be coming up in a
half hour. He had no idea when the slaveowners
would find Jon in a fight with Fred. But he knew
that they could be right behind them. They had
to stop soon. If they did not find somewhere to
hide soon, they would be caught, since horses
were faster than on foot.

As they ran, they arrived at a small creek. On the right side was a seven-foot waterfall. Hasani and Jamilia bent down to get a drink before they went on. Hasani got his drink from the waterfall. He plunged his head in with his mouth open, but he didn't get a drink. He just tasted cold air. He then pulled his head out of the waterfall and turned to Jamilia. He said, "I think there is an open cave behind the waterfall. Hasani jumped into the creek and climbed through the waterfall. The cave was big enough for three grown men. Hasani then slid out of the waterfall and said to Jamilia, "There is a large cave we can stay in for the night. It will keep us hidden from the slaveowners until night falls again."

***

That morning at two o'clock Master Jonathan Hundley woke up hearing a man in agony. He jumped out of bed and ran outside. He was shocked to see his own son, Jon, being beaten by a slave. It looked like his son had been fighting back as best he could, but he was not winning. Somehow, they had been fighting for over an hour. Jon had a purple eye, and his face was covered in blood but he was not dead yet. Fred was bloody as well with a black eye and many bruises. It was clear the slave had the upper hand. Master Hundley quickly woke up all the slave catchers. They all ran out as fast as they could trying to throw on their clothes and grab their guns. They all stumbled outside falling over each other as if they had woken up thirty seconds before. Once they saw the two fighting, they raised their guns. Master Hundley yelled for them not to shoot since he didn't want his son shot. Instead, Master Hundley told them to take the slave and shoot him. The men all scrambled over and threw Fred to the ground.

This finally gave Jon time to rest as he crumbled to the ground.

The group of slavecatchers grabbed Fred and drug him to the whipping wall. This time he was not getting whipped, but he was getting shot. They strapped his hands to the wall and stepped back and aimed all eight guns at his face. Master Hundley then said, "Any last words before you cease from existence?"

Fred hesitated then said, "Dear God, please help me die of the whip, not by the gun." He said it so quietly that none of the men heard it. So, they aimed their guns, and all pulled the trigger. They were only twenty feet away so it would be an easy shot. But out of all eight guns, not one bullet made its mark. Fred thanked God and repeated his request. Again, all the men loaded their guns and pulled the trigger, but again no bullets hit. After both failed attempts

Master Hundley was fuming. He could not understand so he grabbed his whip and whipped Fred till he was almost dead. Then Master Hundley turned him around and was about to whip his face to kill him. Just then Fred put up his hand and in Swahili said, "sisi pia ni watu! rangi ya ngozi yako haipaswi kujali!" Which means, "We are people too! The color of your skin should not matter!" Hundley didn't speak Swahili, and with disgust on his face he brought the whip down hard onto the side of his face. With that, Fred passed from this earth with a smile on his face.

As Master Hundley walked back to his son, the other slavecatchers began conversing on what had just happened. Jon was now being helped by Sarah to get him into the kitchen. She helped him to the couch in the main room and brought warm cloths to clean all his wounds. He had been beaten up way worse than Fred. Jon's left eye was swollen shut and he had a bruise on his right cheek. It was clear that he had lost the fight. Master Hundley, not realizing in the midst of the chaos that two slaves were getting away, stayed by his son's side.

After about an hour and a half, Jon sat up straight. He was full of anger, "Where are the two slaves that were escaping?" Despite the beating he took, the adrenaline coursed through his veins. After hearing no answer but just silence he stood up. His father tried to tell him to rest but Jon said, "Two slaves escaped, and that man risked his life to let them go free. They have been gone for hours. We must find them now!" Master Hundley told him repeatedly that his men were taking care of it, but Jon would not listen. Jon staggered out to the stable and grabbed his horse. Before he left, he opened the hound gate and let all the hounds out. He then swung himself onto his horse. "I will find these

slaves and torture them if it's the last thing I do!"
With that he rode off into the sunrise with a few
of his men and all the dogs following the
Hasani's scent, from a handkerchief of his they
found, after he left.

***

Hasani and Jamilia had scrubbed their
bodies so much in the creek that there was no
way their scent would give them away. Jamilia
had learned to always get to water before you
stopped. Once you got to the water wash well.
Then the dogs could track you that far. But once
in the water the dogs couldn't follow the scent
until you got back on land.

After a few hours in the dark, damp cave,
it began to get cold. Just as Hasani was about to
get a drink he heard horses and hounds coming.
He yanked his head back in the cave and held
Jamilia. She could hear the noises and hear them

talking. As they sat there holding each other she tightened her grip on Hasani.

It felt like hours that they had rested at the creek. The men then all packed up and got ready to move on. They filled up their canteens and were about to leave. Before they left, Jon walked over to the waterfall and stuck his face in the water to get a drink. Hasani could see his nose coming through the waterfall. He wanted to punch it so bad, but he held back his hand. Jon then did pull his head out. Hasani blew a sigh of relief when he realized that he was just getting a drink.

Once they left, Hasani took a breath because he was so tense. He was so glad that they had not been found. They decided not to listen to the people who said travel by night and sleep by day. It would take too long to get to freedom. So, they quietly slipped out from behind the waterfall. Hasani first got out and looked around. Seeing no one, he turned and helped out Jamilia. Just as she landed in the water, they heard a loud dog howl. It wasn't like a wolf howl but a dog howl. Hasani was scared that the dogs had picked up their scent.

Hasani began to walk down the creek and it got bigger like a river. It wasn't too big of a river, but it was up to Hasani's chest. The river was also very brown so it would hide them if they needed to hide quickly. The howl didn't stop which was weird. The howl sounded like the dog was being attacked. Hasani thought that dogs were fighting. He said, "I think it is a fight between a lot of dogs." Jamilia's heart dropped. She had always loved animals and hated it when animals fought, especially when the same animal fought but she couldn't do anything about it, so they trudged through the thick mud on the bottom of the river.

$\mathcal{9}$ Isabella

Jon was riding along trying to keep pressure on his bleeding face. As he was riding again, he saw a black and white border collie. The dog was already starving and very sickly. Jon saw the dog but had no sympathy for the dog. So, he snapped at his dogs, and they attacked the border collie. The howl coming from the dog was so sad, but Jon was cold hearted, and didn't care. When he was a little boy, he had been attacked by a dog, from the command of a slave. When Jon was little his dad still had many slaves, but they would threaten the life of Jon for their freedom from Jon's dad. This was one of the reasons why he hated dogs so much. The only reasons he had his own bloodhound dogs was they could help him catch slaves.

***

As Hasani and Jamilia traveled by the river they began to hear something. It was a sound of rustling in the ferns. It kept happening and it was scaring them because they didn't know what it was.

Finally, they came to a clearing, and saw a young dog stumble into the bushes trying to hide. The dog appeared to be a black and white border collie. The dog was clearly scared of people. Jamilia could see that, so she calmed her voice and said, "Hey there, it's ok. We don't want to hurt you. We are here to help." Hasani could see that this dog had been attacked by a bigger animal. She had scratches all over her body. As Jamilia was looking over the dog, she found that other than just bumps and bruises she was very hungry. Jamilia got up from her knees, took off her pack, dug in it for a bit, and pulled out what she was looking for. It was a can of "Isabella's Cold Beans." As Jamilia opened the can she said, "Well, since we are taking you with us you might as well have a name. What should we call you?" She looked down and she saw the name Isabella. "We will call you Isabella, is that good?"

Isabella looked up at Jamilia as if she was saying, "That's perfect. Thank you for caring for me."

Hasani did not think taking a dog along was a good idea. He didn't see how a dog would be of any use to them. A dog could just slow them down if anything. But Jamilia was happy with the dog and it was good to see her smile for a change. The last time he had seen her perfect smile was when they had first fallen in love that one night on the roof of the slave house.

Jamilia helped Isabella stop bleeding. It had been hard to wash the wounds. Isabella had whimpered a lot due to water getting in her cuts. Jamilia had always loved animals. When she was younger, she would rescue little animals and help them till they were better. That was the reason she and her sister had been kidnapped and sold into slavery.

It all happened one day when they were out rescuing an injured chipmunk. The chipmunk had been attacked by a dog and had a bite in the back. The bite had been small but big enough to put the chipmunk down. It had lost a lot of blood and was dying but Jamilia was doing what she could to save its life. She was only thirteen, but she thought she could save the chipmunk. As she dabbed the blood with her handkerchief the bite began to clean up. But as she finished the cleanup process the chipmunk died. Seeing the dead chipmunk made Jamilia cry. She had tried to save a life of a helpless animal, but she was not able to do it. Her big sister Tiana rolled her eyes. She had never felt the love for little animals like her little sister. But she wanted to be nice, so she bent down and said, "Hey Jamilia it's ok. Chipmunks die all the time." Jamilia looked up inter her big sister's eyes. They were full of love and compassion.

So, Jamilia said, "Yeah, you are right I shouldn't be too sad about it. Let's go home and help mother with dinner. I think she might be making her cookies tonight!" As they were walking home, they began to hear things around them moving like the rustling of bushes and muffled voices. They didn't see anybody, so they kept walking. Suddenly, potato bags were put over their heads. Jamilia was confused at first. She thought it was her sister playing around, but she was wrong. This person was too strong. They were tied up and thrown into a buggy. They both fought, trying to get free. The more they struggled, the tighter the ropes became. Suddenly, a heavy club knocked them both unconscious.

Jamilia remembered how scared she was when she woke up. She remembered how she was in a buggy with thirteen other girls. She scanned every face and finally saw that one girl, who looked like her sister, still had a bag over her head. Jamilia tried moving next to her, but it was hard with all the other girls. With much effort, she was able to get next to her. When she did, she shook Tiana until she began to move. Jamilia helped her sister remove the bag, and when Tiana's eyes met the light, she squinted from the brightness. Tiana then looked down at her hands. Seeing them not tied made her confused. Why had these men untied her? But before she thought any more Jamilia said, "We untied you. We untied all the girls in this buggy." Tiana gave Jamilia a look of appreciation. They had no idea where they were going, but they sensed it was a bad place.

***

Jon had been out for one full day looking for his runaway slaves. He was getting terribly angry. It was about 8:00pm. He and all his men were looking everywhere for these slaves. He absolutely hated Hasani and when he found that he had escaped he determined to dedicate the rest of his life to catching and torturing this man. He had it all planned out how Hasani would be tortured. He would first take his whip which wasn't like the other whips. This one was filled with barbed wire and glass. This would shred the back of Hasani. But that wouldn't be all he would wait till he was sort of healed. Once he was, he would brand him with his cattle mark. After that he would take Hasani apart with an ax, limb by limb till he was dead.

Master Hundley rode up to his son and said, "Let's head back to the house. We can finish this tomorrow and we will find them. Let's get some rest." Jon was angry but he knew his father was right. He lifted his eyes to tell everyone to turn back but he saw a chimney with smoke.

Jon said, "We will check this house then head back. They might be in there." They rode up to the house and tied up their horses. A little old woman came out with a lantern. "Good evening, ma'am, my name is Jon, and we are looking for two runaway slaves. They help us out at our ranch. We absolutely love them, and we thought they loved us too, but they killed one of our men. These two are killers. Have you seen them?" Jon lied.

Anna Walker looked at them with uncertainty. She said, "So they are killers and you loved them? If you loved them then why are your eyes full of hate?"

Jon's demeanor changed, "We are checking your house. Are you going to let us in, or should we do this the hard way?" Mrs. Walker stepped out of the doorway and let them in. Jon rushed in the house and began looking in every nook and cranny. He did not find one sign of slaves being in the house.

After a half hour of searching Jon finally walked out of the house. Mrs. Walker followed him, and Jon said, "I am leaving one of my men here at this house just in case they come here."

Mrs. Walker said, "That's fine with me because I would never rescue a killer." With that Jon rode back to his house with all his men but William Turner. William was left to make sure she never hid a slave. Since he had been riding all day, he was tired, so he walked to the main room. There was Mrs. Walker sitting in her rocking chair sewing a quilt. Will told her to get out of the chair. Once she stood up, he sat down, kicked back his feet, and fell asleep.

Mrs. Walker began to clean up the house. She told herself, "I would never take in a killer. But I never said anything about taking in slaves who have a good reason." She then turned towards the man who was trying to sleep, and she said, "I am getting water at the river."

In the back there was a deck that overlooked the river. She had a very beautiful view. There was a nice sandy beach below her deck and there was a big waterfall about five miles upriver, so the river wasn't too fast down here. The sunset was straight ahead, and the sun was just beginning to slip behind the mountains. This gave the sky a beautiful color just before the sun disappeared.

The man jumped up and said, "We will see about that. I am following you." The man followed her down to the river, but she wasn't lying. She was getting water. So, the man walked back up to the house and went in. As Mrs. Walker turned to follow, she saw something in the reeds by the beach. When she saw what it was, she ran over and picked it up. Her eyes went wide with shock.

***

As Hasani and Jamilia waded through the water, it began to get colder by the minute. Jamilia was freezing cold from the water; she had no food or clean water. She had given the last of their food to Isabella So, she hurried up through the water to Hasani who then put his arm around her. But feeling her frozen arms he took off his jacket and put it on Jamilia. This now left him with a thin work shirt.

When Jamilia saw what he was wearing she rejected the jacket. She was wearing a sweater, but it was wet, and it was colder. Hasani had given up his only warmth. The shirt would do nothing for him. Jamilia pleaded with him, "You need to keep this. That shirt you are wearing will not save you. You will get too cold if we continue through this river." But Hasani, being the gentleman that he was, refused to take back the jacket.

As they trudged on, the water got colder and colder. Ahead, Hasani could hear a waterfall and he stopped by a pile of rocks. Jamilia moved over to them and climbed up. Hasani began to do the same then he said, "We will need to get..." But before he could finish his sentence, he was pulled under water. Jamilia screamed in terror as she peered into the murky water. She looked but didn't see any sign of him. He finally came up downstream, it was clear the current had caught him. He was flailing his arms trying to find something to grab hold of. There were no rocks or tree branches to grab. Jamilia climbed out of the river and ran down the river with Isabella, trying to find a way to save him.

Jamilia then saw a rock dam coming up. But it was only over half the river so it wouldn't stop Hasani. She ran as fast as she possibly could and slowly got onto the dam. As she slowly walked on, she could hear rocks shifting underneath her. She knew it wouldn't hold her so she turned to Isabella and told her what to do. She then prayed a quick prayer and told Isabella to go. Isabella crept onto the dam and when she got to the end of the dam, she could see Hasani coming up fast. He would pass inches in front of her. So, when he reached her, she sprang into action. She reached out her teeth and bit into his shirt. Once she had that secure, she hooked the shirt to a rock on the dam. She had to use all the strength she had left to do it. Now that he was hooked the dam began to shake. Hasani looked around and found a large log that was a part of the dam. So, he put his hands on that. This was so if the dam broke, he would have a log to hold onto and maneuver back to shore with.

In only seconds, the dam sprung a leak due to too much weight on it. Because the log was so big it was harder to be pushed by the water, so it floated to the shore. When he climbed onto land, Jamilia ran over to him and forced the jacket onto him. This time he took it gladly. He was freezing cold. There were parts of his body that had gone completely numb to the water. Hasani then turned around quickly to see the dam break and Isabella look into his eyes with a look of fear. He walked back out into the water to try and save the dog that saved his life, but the current was too strong, and he couldn't save her. Hasani was sad and thought that Jamilia would be devastated but she said, "I am comforted that you are ok. It is sad that Isabella didn't make it, but I love you much more than the dog." Hasani could tell she was still sad though. Right then he promised to get her a dog just like Isabella when they became free.

***

As Mrs. Walker reached into the reeds, she picked up a soaking and what appeared to be a dead dog. She burst into tears because of how much she loved dogs. But she wouldn't give up hope, and brought the dog back up to the house. As she was walking up, she saw someone hiding behind the woodpile. She stopped walking and quietly said, "Right behind you is an entrance to an underground room. You may stay there as long as you want. I will bring food later tonight. I am here to keep you safe. Please do as I say and when I stamp my foot twice on the ground you need to get out and into the river. That means that someone is here looking for slaves to kill. There is a man upstairs who cannot see you or he will kill you, so stay silent."

The hiding man said, "Thank you so much. You'll never know how much this means to me."

10 Safe Haven

Hasani and Jamilia continued down the river but this time they kept their feet in the water. They didn't want their footprints to be seen or their scent to be tracked. After a few minutes of walking, Hasani began to shiver aggressively. There was no doubt that hypothermia was setting in. The heat there in Alabama was bad, but the wintertime was brutal, and the water was now very cold.

After about three miles of walking, they saw a light up ahead. As they neared, it looked like a house, and they knew they had to find shelter. If they didn't try or ask at all to have a place to stay and to hide, Hasani would die of hypothermia and Jamilia knew she couldn't and wouldn't be able to go on without him. If they went in the house and the homeowner sent them back to their slave plantation, they wouldn't be killed but worse. They would be tortured for running away. Hasani swore that he would never go back to that slave place. He hated every second of it. He would kill himself before they got there. Whatever it was, he would not go back to being a slave owned by Jon Hundley.

Jamilia began to think of the different possibilities that could happen. First of all, she had heard rumors of the door. The door was painted red. She wasn't sure but she thought that she had heard somewhere that if the door was red that meant it was a safe house. She knew that if the owner of the house sent them back then they would be tortured to death. But, if she was going to die, then she knew that she would be spending the rest of her life with her Savior. She also would be able to meet Moses and the slaves of Egypt in heaven. The only sensible option was to risk it and ask for a place to stay. She knew they had to try. She knew she had to stand strong and hope that she was right about the door. If they didn't, they both would die. Thinking about death made her think of Isabella. She had undoubtably died due to the cold and drowned. There was basically no chance of survival. It was sad, but Jamilia could do nothing about it.

As they approached the house, they saw a little old lady cleaning up through the window by the door. The sun was just setting behind the mountains, so it gave a dark look to everything. Jamilia could hardly see anything, just a darkening orange sky. There was only half a candle stick lit inside on the table. Hasani walked up to the door and knocked quietly. He then stepped back off the porch to wait for the answer. Seconds later, the door opened a crack and the woman peered out. When she saw the figures in front of her, she closed the door.

Mrs. Walker closed the door and looked back into the kitchen. Seeing that Will was fast asleep on the rocking chair, she slipped outside. When the door latched shut, the eyes of William snapped open.

Anna Walker held up the lantern to their faces of the two figures and a wave of compassion went across her face. She whispered and said, "I am Mrs. Anna Walker. I am here to rescue you. I am a part of the underground railroad. Please go around to the back deck. There is a room under the deck. It has an underground tunnel that leads into it. The entrance to the tunnel is under the stack of wood. When you have put all your things away, I will give you food. Please be quiet there is someone here who shouldn't see you."

Just as she said that out loud, Hasani thanked her but was cut off by her telling him to stay quiet. It was too late. The man walked out the door behind Mrs. Walker. When he saw Hasani, his eyes became filled with anger. He ran at Hasani ready to throw a punch, but Hasani got out of the way and the man missed. Hasani dropped his jacket and bag and was ready for a fight. This fight would warm him up since he was still cold. Although he had become numb, he forced himself to fight. Jamilia walked over to Mrs. Walker and looked her in the face and snapped, "How could you invite us in just to have us captured. I cannot believe you would do this to people. We are people too. Why do you treat us so badly?" Mrs. Walker tried to protest but Jamilia wouldn't let her. She grabbed

Hasani's bag and began to leave, expecting Hasani to follow.

But Hasani did not follow. He wasn't ready to leave. He had a fight to finish. Hasani landed many perfect punches and kicks and William landed a few. They fought for so long and Hasani had hypothermia, so he began to get cold again. The sweat was cold, and he was freezing. This gave the man the upper hand and he began beating up Hasani. Just as he had Hasani up against the wall and was ready to punch him hard to end it all, something hit the man in the back of the head. This made him drop to the ground. There standing behind him was Mrs. Anna Walker.

Hasani walked over to the woman and looked her in the eye. He raised an eyebrow as if he were shocked. In a quiet, low voice, he said, "Why would you knock him out if you wanted us caught? Or were you telling us the truth this entire time?"

Mrs. Anna calmly said, "He was forced to stay here. I didn't make him stay. I will help every runaway slave that asks." Hasani let out a sigh of relief as he realized that she really was telling the truth.

"Can you take us inside and give us something to eat?" Hasani asked.

Mrs. Walker's heart felt nothing but pity and compassion and said, "Of course, please come in and I will give you food and a warm bed to sleep in. But first we must find a place for this man."

As Jamilia followed Mrs. Walker into the house, she was surprised at what she saw. She ran in past Mrs. Walker and did not stop. Hasani then saw what Jamilia had found, and he felt a warm feeling inside. There, lying next to the fire, wrapped up in a towel, was Isabella, very much alive! Jamilia hugged the dog so much Hasani thought Isabella would be choked to death, but she was just as excited to see the familiar faces.

After the joyous reunion, Anna Walker gestured for them to sit down at the table. Jamilia quickly did so. Hasani leaned Will against the wall. He lost consciousness and would not remember anything when he woke up. Hasani then sat down next to Jamilia.

As Anna turned to prepare food, a wave of terrible memories flooded through her mind. Memories of how her husband had been killed by a runaway slave. She had every right to get revenge on slaves and kill them. But she just couldn't send another human being through pain because she was angry. She also knew that no matter how mad she got she had to live with the realization that her husband wasn't coming back.

Anna ladled some stew into bowls for the both of them. She always made more stew than she needed because she knew slaves could arrive at any time. She then filled a basket of bread and turned around. As she sat down, she struck up conversation. "So where are you headed?"

Hasani shot his head up still pretty paranoid, "Why do you want to know? Why are you helping us and how did you find our dog Isabella?"

Anna sat down, threw her hands in the air and said, "Woah, there. I can't answer all that at the same time. But I can answer them one at a time. Let's start with the first. I want to know where you are going so that I can point you in the right direction. I know where every house is on

155

this underground railroad. I am helping you because that is what my husband always wanted before he died, by the hands of a runaway slave."

Hasani looked up quickly and said, "Your husband was killed by a slave?"

Anna looked back at him and said, "Yes he was. It was a night like tonight. He was out hunting for food. He had always wanted to help slaves escape. While he was hunting, he found a bear and tracked it for hours. He finally found it drinking by our house. As he snuck closer and aimed the gun, he looked at it and saw a slave on the other side of the river. The bear was somewhat hidden, so the slave looked up and saw him holding the gun at him. My husband then put down the gun and called him over. He swam across the river still not noticing the bear. The slave then walked out of the water. Just as he was ten feet away the bear came out behind the slave. Then my husband, wanting to rescue the man, raised his gun to the bear. But the slave only thought he was killing him, so he attacked my husband. He threw him to the ground before he could tell him. The runaway slave grabbed the gun and shot my husband. The bear ran towards the slave and killed him too! I watched all this happen from my window and was petrified with fear."

As she told them, tears fell down her cheeks. Hasani was stunned, "Why would you help us if your husband was killed by one of us?"

Anna then stopped crying and said sternly, "Are you that slave who killed my husband? No, you are a different person. Why should I kill anyone just because they have darker skin? We are all human beings and should all be treated the same. Whether black, white, or even green skinned, you are still a human who was made by God. The God who made you also made me. I will never kill another human, no matter the color."

Hasani knew that everything she was saying was true. He also knew that Will would wake soon, so they had to be on the move. He stood and said, "Well, we should get going. Thank you for everything that you have..."

"No, you will not be leaving. I have a cabin under this house that is fully hidden. You will stay the night tonight and head out tomorrow night. Your things are already here so you can just stay the night," Anna interrupted.

Hasani was stunned by how well hidden the lower room was. There was no sign of the room being there. You would only know from in the house if you crawled under the bed and moved a box. Under the box was a tunnel that led to the bigger room. The bigger room was big enough to hold ten grown men.

Hasani climbed down the ladder he looked around as he lit the lantern. What he saw, took his breath away and his body froze like a statue.

11 United

Hasani stopped moving and froze, like a statue. Jamilia urged him to move out of the way, but he wouldn't budge. She was finally able to squeeze past him and when she saw what he saw she was dumbfounded. She ran over and jumped on the bed where a man was sleeping. The man lying there was his presumed dead, best friend Hashim! Jamilia awoke him and he sat up with a start. When he saw that it was Jamilia and Hasani he broke down crying and said, "I thought I'd never see you again!"

Hasani finally broke free from his trance and started spitting questions at him. "I thought you died. How did you get here? Did you come alone? Who helped you with your wounds?"

Hashim said, "Slow down and let's get some sleep. Tomorrow, we leave. I will share all in time." Hasani agreed and gave Hashim a big hug. Hashim said, "You and Jamilia sleep on the bed, I will sleep on the ground tonight. Now, we rest."

When Hasani woke up a few hours later, he sat up. He began to shake Jamilia and when she was awake, he got out of bed as quickly as he could. Jamilia watched him run around trying to make sense of everything. She chuckled then said, "Hasani, we are in Anna Walker's house. She is keeping us safe remember?"

Hasani stopped and an embarrassed smirk came across his face. He said, "Oh yeah, sorry about that. I completely forgot where we were."

Hashim just sat in the corner chuckling and said, "You haven't changed one bit, have you.

Hasani got dressed and ready for their big day of travel. When they were all packed and prepared to leave, they climbed up the ladder to the trap door. Hasani pushed up the on the trap door, but it was locked. That woman had locked them in the underground cell! They had trusted her! This must be part of her plan; she played the part, helped slaves and captured them. Fuming, the three slaves discussed their situation.

Jamilia actually felt bad for the woman. She couldn't believe that she had been fooled. Her eyes seemed too sincere for Jamilia not to believe. She even rescued Isabella, a woman who hates slaves couldn't be nice enough to rescue drowning dogs, could they? Jamilia didn't know what to think. Hasani paced the room trying to think of a logical explanation. But the only thing he would believe was she had turned on them. Hashim then said, "There is another exit out of here. she did not turn on us, she is trustworthy." Hasani looked up and saw the tunnel to the stack of wood. This was the original entrance that they would have used if there wasn't a fight. Hasani quickly grabbed his pack and they all climbed out.

When they reached the outside of the tunnel, they could tell it was early in the morning. The fog was just lifting, and the candles were lit in the house. Hasani looked in a window and saw Mrs. Walker drinking coffee at the table. Hasani, Hashim and Jamilia crept closer to the window and peered in. Hasani's heart dropped. There at the other side of the table was the man he had fought yesterday. It looked like he didn't remember a thing. He was just sitting there, drinking out of a mug. Hasani stumbled back a step. He wasn't about to get into another fight. Just before he turned to leave. He caught Mrs. Walker's eye. Hasani could see that she wanted him to leave. So, he turned and walked away. Just as Jamilia turned around, Mrs. Walker stood up and walked to the door. Jamilia ran and they hid behind a tree. Watching from behind the tree they saw as Mrs. Walker open the door. Through the door walked Hasani's nightmare. He was going to have to fight again. But then Isabella ran out the door and sat on the porch. The man and Mrs. Walker then went inside.

Once the door closed, Isabella ran to Hasani and Jamilia. Hasani and Jamilia were so happy that they had been reunited. With that they continued on their way. Everyone was feeling much better to be able to be on the move with Hashim.

Right after they had begun walking Hashim said, "So Hasani, you've got a new best friend? At least tell me his name?"

Hasani laughed, "Sorry but everyone knows a dog is man's best friend. Didn't mean to replace you or anything. We also thought you were dead so I needed someone" Hasani said sarcastically.

12 Halfway to Freedom

As Jon and his men woke up that day, he felt a wave of anger come over him as he was saddled his horse. His mind replayed back how his father had given control of the farm to the hands of Adam for a few weeks. Just thinking about possibly losing the control of the farm to Adam from his own father made him swear underneath his breath. Jon angrily saddled his horse and left for another full day of searching. He knew that if he found this slave and brought him back, he might regain control of the farm.

**

The runaways had now been on the move from Mrs. Walker's house for about five hours.

It was hard to walk this long. They were very tired, and knew they should stop soon. Conversation with constant with Hashim which helped pass the time. Hashim explained that he awoke from being unconscious, lying in the river and was chilled to the bone. He stood up to run, but fell to the ground. His feet were so frozen he couldn't feel them at all. It was snowing and the air had gotten much colder out. He was able to manage his walking difficulties while leaning on a stick. There was so much pain, but he knew he had to keep moving. He finally came to a house, but didn't want to risk it, so he hid in the wood pile by the house. Now that he was out of the snow, he was able to rest. Minutes after arriving, a woman and a man walked out of the house. Hashim ducked down lower so he wouldn't be seen because he didn't know if they were friend or foe. After a few steps, the man turned around and stomped back inside. The woman filled up a bucket of water from her well. She then stopped and reached behind the wood pile. Hashim panicked because he thought he had dropped something out of his pockets. The woman slowly turned looked him square in the eyes. Hashim panicked, but she calmed him down by whispering to him that there was a trap door underneath him and it led to an underground room, in which he would be safe for the night.

Hashim also caught up on how Hasani escaped with Jamilia, and they told him the long story in great detail. Hasani knew they had to be hidden when they stopped. If they just rested in a tree, they would be found. But being in a house the scent was harder track. That would be having them stop at around six. Hasani still had the gold pocket watch so he knew the time. He was thankful that his father had taught he and his brother how to read a clock.

As they hiked, their discussion transitioned to spiritual things. Hasani shared that he hadn't been a good man of God although he had promised to be a servant to God and to follow him fully. Hashim was disappointed that his death hadn't led Hasani to following Christ, but instead sent him spiraling farther from God. They were so close as friends and Hasani didn't take it to heart when Hashim and Jamilia talked to him about God. He knew he wasn't interested, and was sure nothing would change that. Hasani's mind was set on escaping to freedom. Any outside distractions, even if they were spiritual, would just slow them down. He knew they had been walking for a long time and the pursuers would catch up in the next few hours. So, they had to find an overnight stay.

Jamilia felt relieved that Mrs. Walker had not turned on them. She did not see her as a woman who could be so mean. There was sincerity in her voice. Jamilia was also happy that she had Isabella back. The dog was healthy and had been well taken care of by Mrs. Walker.

As Hasani hiked on he felt his legs getting more and more tired by the minute. Hashim wasn't doing much better. It was obvious that his feet hadn't completely healed from being frozen. He was stumbling about. Jamilia saw them grow more and more exhausted. Jamilia grabbed Hasani by the arm and began helping him along.

All of a sudden, Hasani dropped to the ground. As Jamilia was helping Hasani, Hashim dropped. They both had fainted of exhaustion. Hasani had been through so much and it was taking a toll on his body. Jamilia tried repeatedly to wake him, but he would not wake. Just then it began to snow hard. Not just regular snow but blizzard type snow. When it seemed that things couldn't get worse, it did.

Jamilia began crying and vigorously shaking him to try to get him up, but it was no use. Jamilia then began trying to drag him but he was so heavy and Jamilia was very tired as well. Jamilia worked for quite some time, trying to drag and trying to wake up either of the men, but it was no use. She couldn't do it. She had lost all her energy that the only thing she could do was just lay down and rest. Isabella tried helping but there was not much a dog could do. Then, just as Jamilia thought she had lost all hope, Isabella ran off. Jamilia tried to tell her to come back but she wouldn't. Jamilia knew if she didn't move, she would get hypothermia, but she was too tired to move. With that she fell unconscious, in the middle of the forest in a terrible blizzard.

When Jamilia awoke, she sat up and looked around. She was lying in an enormous bed. Next to her, lay her love. Hasani was breathing which gave Jamilia a relief of gladness. Seeing this she got out of bed and walked around. The room was exceptionally large and there was a walk-in closet in the corner. The door was open to the room, so she quietly creeped out into a large church building.

The room had many rows of pews. There were ten rows back and four rows wide. The windows all were beautifully crafted stained glass. On the windows were images of a figure who did many different things. In one window was a mother, father and a baby in a barn. In another, there was a man hung on a cross on a hill. These images on the windows brought a sorrow of heart to Jamilia. Thinking of the Bible it became clear that the man was Jesus. There also were pictures of black people being treated with love by Jesus. She had learned all about Jesus in church but had never seen pictures like this.

There was a large stage in the front and a pulpit in the middle. Their rescuer must have been either the pastor or someone who worked in the church. Just as she was about to turn back into the room, she heard a voice. The voice was calm and full of compassion. The voice said, "Look who finally awoke from her deep sleep."

Jamilia turned around to see a tall slender man. He had a short goatee of a beard, and he was dressed as if he was a pastor. Jamilia stepped forward instinctively to shake his hand. But then stepped back because she knew nothing about him.

"You have been asleep for almost forty-eight hours. It was a good thing we found you all when we did. If we didn't find you when we did your husband would have died of pneumonia and hypothermia."

Jamilia then said quietly, "Thank you for rescuing us. What did you say your name was?"

"Oh, my name is Reverend Edward Johnston."

Jamilia smiled then continued, "Who are you and are we safe here with you?"

The reverend's eyes brightened and said, "I am the Reverend of Sinking Creek Baptist Church here in Johnson City, Tennessee. Where are you both from?" Jamilia was too astonished to respond. They were over halfway to freedom. She had known this because she had seen maps before she went into slavery. He father had taught both his daughters the route until they knew it well. If they reached freedom alive, they would be a part of the few percent to survive escaping bondage.

Rev. Johnston then said, "Church will be starting in one hour so I must go. I would want you to join the service, but sadly, there are some in my church who would report you. If you stay in that room, you will be safe."

The room they had been in, was kind of like a guest room for the church. Jamilia turned and went to Hasani's side by the bed. Isabella ran to her as she opened the door. Jamilia rubbed her behind the back of her head and this made her tail wag vigorously. Hearing the dog's movements, Hashim shifted the blankets in a chair that he was sleeping in. Hasani was just getting up from his long sleep. The first thing he saw was Jamilia's beautiful face.

Hasani looked at her with a confused look and asked, "What happened and where are we?"

Jamilia smiled and said, "You blacked out for a long time. I think I just fell asleep. But a pastor here rescued us. And there is more good news! We are in Tennessee! That means we are over halfway to freedom. We just must get into Indiana, and we are free. But we must move fast. Tennessee has many who would turn us over. I overheard men at the plantation saying that Tennessee was great for them because over half of white people hate blacks."

Hasani was now in a sitting position pondering everything that was being said. Just as Hasani was about to respond they heard some music playing. Hearing the songs made them happy. The last time they heard music was about a month before in church. Jamilia was surprised that white men were singing the same familiar song that they did. The song was "Jesus Paid it All" by Elvina Hall. Jamilia then began quietly humming along with the song. Hasani had never heard or even noticed the words to this song. He had heard this tune sung in church and in the fields, but he hadn't heard the actual words. He listened to the whole song and contemplated all of it. He loved all the verses in the song, but he most loved the chorus which said:

Jesus paid it all,

All to Him I owe.

Sin had left a crimson stain,

He washed it white as snow.

The words really stuck out to him as he thought about what that meant. Jesus paid it all? What did that mean? He washed it white as snow. Who did that and what is sin that was washed away? He had so many questions, but they were questions for a man of faith to answer. Hasani also needed to ask a minister a favor.

13 New Life

After the church service had finished, Hasani cracked open the door. Seeing that there was nobody in the room he opened it the rest of the way and motioned for Jamilia to come out.

They emerged from the small corner room into the large sanctuary. Hashim stayed behind because he wanted to sleep in the bed that Hasani and Jamilia had been in. He slept all night, but on a chair in the corner. The room was the most beautiful structure that Hasani had ever seen. He loved all the stained-glass windows. They walked towards the stage and looked at the room.

Just then Reverend Johnston walked in reading some papers. Hasani stepped back and grabbed Jamilia's hand by reflex. Jamilia whispered to him that it was ok and that he was nice. The man walked down the aisle, when he got about halfway, he looked up from his reading. He smiled the two standing at the stage and walked towards them folding his papers. Hasani raised his voice and said, "Who are you and what do you want?"

But the man smiled and said, "I rescued you from the cold outside. I do want you to stay a few days and get ready for the long journey ahead of you, but you will need to be on your way tomorrow. I have a friend who lives on the border of Indiana and Kentucky. There is a train about three miles west of here. I can get you on a cargo boxcar. The train has one stop before reaching Indiana. It stops at the border and the slave patrol search the train. So, you will need to

180

get off before then. I don't want to risk sending you by train into Indiana because the slave patrol search trains for slaves before entering the freedom state. I am sorry but this is the only way to get you to freedom. Now let's get you some food and some more rest before tomorrow." He then turned around and motioned for them to follow him.

Hasani followed him to the door with Jamilia by his side. Rev. Johnston held the door for them and let them through. Before Hasani walked through he stopped and looked at the reverend. He then asked, "Are you a man who knows God? Because I need to talk to a man who can talk to God."

Rev. Johnston looked at him with joy saying, "You can talk to God too."

Jamilia sat down with Rev. Johnston's young triplets. Andrew, Anthony, and Arthur were all six years old. Watching the kids play made her think about having her own children one day. She knew that she wanted children, but she hadn't talked to Hasani about it.

Hasani sat in a pew with Rev. Johnston talking about things of God. Hasani never paid attention in his old church. But today he was listening to Rev. Johnston tell him the entire story of his Savior. The summary of what he was saying was this: A long time ago a baby named Jesus Christ was born in Bethlehem in a stable. He was sent to the world by God to save everyone from their sin. Jesus grew up as a perfect man. That mean that he never sinned. Although he was tempted, he never sinned. As Jesus got older, he traveled with his disciples healing sick and giving sight to the blind. By the power of his Father in heaven he was able to perform miracles. But there were people called the Pharisees. They were like the government;

they oversaw the making of laws. When they saw what Jesus was doing, they began to hate him. They did not like him because he said He was the Christ which to them was called blasphemy. Over time they tried to find ways to get rid of him but to no avail. Finally, they found a way to crucify him. The disciple, Judas Iscariot, was able to sell Jesus to be crucified for thirty pieces of silver. One-night Jesus took his disciples to a garden to spend time praying. Jesus prayed alone repeatedly but later he was betrayed by Judas and was taken away by soldiers of Pilate. The soldiers took him and crucified him on a cross. He was killed and he took the killing willingly. Jesus knew that to save the world he would have to give up his life and die.

But it didn't end there. Jesus died and three days later something marvelous happened. In the morning three women went to the sealed tomb and saw that the rock had been rolled away, but not by human hands. That rock was too heavy for any human to move. It took a few men to move it. Sitting on the stone was an angel who said, "Do not be afraid, for I know that you are looking for Jesus, who was crucified. He is not here; he has risen, just as he said. Come and see the place where he lay." Jesus then went to heaven to prepare a home for us. Jesus will come back one day and take us all to heaven to live with him. Jesus not only died for our sins, but he conquered death showing his power.

"It's like in the song we sang today 'Jesus Paid it all,' that, Hasani, is the story of my Savior. Jesus wants to be your Savior, but you have to let him into your heart. If you let him into your heart that gives you a personal relationship with Jesus. Do you want to let him into your heart today?"

Hasani looked up and into the compassionate eyes of his new friend. Hasani then said, "For all of my life I have neglected church. I have not been the man of God Jamilia needed me to be and I have not been a faithful servant to Jesus Christ. I want to be his servant and let him into my heart." The reverend smiled then prayed with him. When the reverend finished praying, he told Hasani to talk to God and ask him to come into his heart.

Hasani then bowed his head and said, "Jesus I know that I am a sinner like all humans. But I do not want to be a bad man later in life. I want to be honorable to my future children. I also want to be a servant again, but not a servant to an earthly master but a servant to you God. Like Hashim said in the letter to me when he told me to be your servant and let you be my master. Jesus, please come inside of me and make me worthy to be your servant." After Hasani had finished his prayer, he lifted his head and looked at the reverend with tear-stained eyes. He felt a smile grow on his face. He felt a wave of joy and unspeakable gladness come over him. When Hasani calmed down, the reverend gave him a small pocket New Testament Bible. This he could take with him everywhere. Just before he was about to leave the room he said, "Reverend, may I ask you another question? I need to talk to you, and it is important."

Later that day, Hasani found Jamilia looking through the church library. She had been there for a long time. Jamilia loved books since she had been taught to read as a young girl. Hasani walked up to her and called out her name. She turned and looked at him. When she looked into his eyes, she saw his joy and she threw her arms around him. She just knew that he had finally accepted a new lifelong master.

The most life changing moment was that evening when he was sitting in the pew with Hashim. Hasani had asked Hashim to come talk to him. Hasani broke their silence and said, "So today I talked with the reverend, and he said some very convicting things. We talked a lot about Christ, and he told me the whole story. At first, I wasn't too excited about it but the more he talked the more it intrigued me. So, I prayed with the reverend and asked Jesus to come into my heart so that I could have a personal relationship with Christ."

Hashim stood up abruptly. Hasani thought he had angered Hashim and said, "Wait, what's wrong? I thought you wanted this." Hashim turned around and had tears on his eyes. Hasani had almost never seen Hashim cry, and he was comforted by the love and support Hashim had for him..

Hashim said, "I am not mad, and I could never be mad about this. It's an answer to every prayer of mine! I have prayed for you ever since I first met you when I was a little kid. I am so overjoyed, and I promise God will never ever let you down." They embraced in the tightest hug. These two were, as close as two friends can be. Close enough to even be called brothers.

14 Two Become One

Jon and his men had now been riding around on their horses for three days. They had just reached the old woman's house again. He had left one of his men there to see if anyone had stopped by. Jon walked up to the porch and pounded on the door. Mrs. Walker opened the door and Jon stepped in and walked over to Will. Will stood up and put down his cup of coffee on the table he was sitting at. Will reported that no one had shown up. But after he had told him that he then thought back and said that he blacked out the other day and woke up not remembering anything. Jon puzzled over this and paced the room. A moment later he walked into the kitchen where Mrs. Walker was baking bread.

He grabbed her by the shoulder and spun her around. Looking into her eyes he asked, "Did you take in any slaves in the last three days? If you do not tell me, we will search your house until it has been checked everywhere!" Mrs. Walker did not say anything. She just looked down. Jon walked away and threw a pitcher through her back window which startled her.

"Search the house until we find something. Don't leave any blanket unturned!" He commanded. His three, now four men who were with him spread out to start searching. Jon did not leave the room, he stayed to keep an eye on Mrs. Walker. After about half an hour one of Jon's men came out of the bedroom and said that he found something. Jon rushed into Mrs. Walkers bedroom and looked around. The man told him it was under the bed. Jon dropped down to the floor and looked. He stood up and looked at Mrs. Walker and smiled a sly smile. He dropped back to the floor and crawled under the bed. Seeing a box over half of the trapdoor he pushed it away. He said, "Push the bed to the left!" The other men standing around moved the bed to reveal a trapdoor that had been under a wood box.

He opened the trapdoor and walked down into the basement. He stepped down the creaky steps and told his men to wait upstairs. When he got to the bottom he looked around. There was a box of matches and a lantern. He lit the lantern and checked the room. He saw a small room with one twin bed. The bed was not made and there was a blanket on the floor. There was a pitcher and bowl overturned on the floor. The walls were dirt and the room looked like it was used. There were no cobwebs or bugs. It was thoroughly cleaned like it was a guest room. Seeing this he came to the obvious conclusion that Mrs. Walker lied to him. Jon walked up the steps.

When he reached the main room one of his men asked, "What was down there? Are the slaves down there?"

Jon looked at the man who said that and retorted, "Does it look like there were the slaves down there? If they were down there, don't you think I would have told you already? Do you understand, Mrs. Walker? They will not just die quickly there will be much suffering. We will also kill you for holding these slaves in your home, you will tell us which way they went. If you don't, then we will kill you and burn down your house. So, tell me which way they went?" he snarled. Mrs. Walker did not answer, she would not give in and tell them.

Jon chuckled and turned around walked over to the mantle. On the mantle was a picture of a young Anna Walker and her husband at her wedding so many years ago. Jon grabbed the picture frame and smashed the glass on the corner of table. This startled Mrs. Walker, and her eyes began to tear up. Jon grabbed the picture out of it and ripped it in half. He then threw it on the ground and stomped on it. Mrs. Walker now had tears flowing down her cheeks. Jon, seeing this, walked over, and pulled out his knife. Putting it to her neck he asked her again. "TELL ME NOW WHERE THEY WENT!" Mrs. Walker flinched at his yelling but wouldn't tell him. Jon knew she would give in soon. He spun around in frustration. "DESTROY EVERYTHING!" Make her talk! So, his men began to break things in the room. They threw chairs through the windows. They ripped blankets and broke bookshelves.

"STOP!!! They were going north. They are heading to Indiana. I promise that is all I know!" Anna cried out.

Jon smiled and told his men to follow him. They ran out of the house, but before they left, they set the house ablaze consuming Mrs. Walker and all she owned. Jon rode away laughing. But something in his heart hurt doing that to another human. He knew deep down how sweet she seemed. But he knew he was too full of rage. He also didn't want to be found out that it was him, so he kept riding.

***

Jamilia began making her bed and putting her extra clothes in her bag. As she finished packing Hasani came in and said, "Hey" startling Jamilia.

She laughed and said, "Don't do that again. You know I hate getting jump scared." Hasani then put a hand on her shoulder and she turned around.

She looked into his eyes, and he said, "I talked to the reverend just now and he told me things about God. He told me about how Jesus is the Son of God came to earth and died for our sins. I believe that now and I am sorry for not listening to you about this in the past." Jamilia threw her arms around him with joy and kissed him. Hasani looked at her. Jamilia feeling embarrassed, looked down at her feet. But Hasani wasn't finished talking. He began again, "I also talked with him about something else. I feel like you mean a lot to me which is why I want to marry you. What I am trying to say is will you get married to me in ten minutes?"

Jamilia looked up with tears in her eyes. She looked at Hasani and said "YES." Hasani embraced her in a passionate kiss and said, "I am going to go get ready, so meet me down in the sanctuary in ten minutes. The reverend will be waiting." Hasani ran to the reverend who was holding up a black suit. Hasani said, "I can't wear that. It's yours."

The reverend stopped him and said, "This is the most important day of your life. You will wear it."

As Hasani walked back into the sanctuary, he joined the reverend on stage. The reverend had also gone to all the trouble of putting on his Sunday best. Hasani shook hands with him and stood next to the reverend with Hashim as well. Hashim leaned over and said, "From the first day you met Jamilia, I was

hoping I would be able to come to the wedding."
Hearing that made Hasani laugh.

It had been the first time in a long time
that Hasani had not only laughed but genuinely
been joyful. He then turned and looked as the
back door opened. Hasani's was stunned at what
he saw. He did not know that the reverend had a
white wedding dress. Later he found out that the
reverend's wife had given Jamilia her old
wedding dress. This was too much for Hasani
and he tried to hold back the tears.

Reverend Johnston put his hand on his
shoulder and said, "It's ok. You can cry."
Hasani heard this and just let the tears fall. As
Jamilia got closer, he could see that she had teary
eyes as well. When Jamilia reached the stage,
she turned and held his hands. They went
through the wedding vows. Hasani did
everything that the reverend asked but he was

lost in the eyes of his beloved. Finally, the reverend said the most precious words of the entire day, "I now pronounce you man and wife. You may kiss the bride." Hasani leaned forward and Jamilia did as well, and they became Mr. and Mrs. Hasani Davis.

15 Train Ride

The morning after Hasani and Jamilia officially became married they packed up and prepared to head to the next location. They had stayed in the hidden room at the church for one more night. The hike to the train was only three miles. It wouldn't be too hard. The hard part would be getting on the cargo train without anyone seeing them. Hasani had a small plan, but as he thought it through, he began to doubt that it would work. The hike was through a very thick forest that seemed like it would not end. It was also very foggy that early in the morning. Hasani kept hearing noises. He thought they were horses, but he wasn't sure. He realized he must be still tired, and still being tired must have made his mind play tricks on him. They hiked at an average speed. They would not run because they would have less reaction time. If they ran, they would be heard. But if they walked, they were quieter.

Every minute Hasani would spin around looking in every direction. He didn't know for sure if it was his mind or if it was real. He kept hearing horses walk around and the horses would neigh. Finally, Jamilia turned around and grabbed his hand. He looked at her and she said, "It's gonna be ok. Nobody is following us we are too far." Hasani just took a deep breath, gripped her hand and continued their way through the foggy forest.

After about twenty minutes they saw the small loading dock. The train was stopped and they were loading some things onto the train. The runaways were standing atop hill heading to the loading dock. They were able to see for miles. There were not many trees and it was just very flat from there. There also was a town about two miles down. Hasani, Jamilia and Isabella ran down to the train. Hasani looked around and saw a boxcar with no lock. So, he ducked behind a bush and told Jamilia and Hashim his plan. Jamilia didn't think it was the best plan, but she didn't have a better one, so she went with it.

The plan was they would one by one starting with Jamilia and Isabella, run to the train and crawl under laying on the tracks. The Hashim would go after them. Then Hasani would go last and he would go open the boxcar and everyone would get in and then close the door behind them. Remembering what the reverend said was they would have to get off the train before it got to the station. So, they would have to jump off a moving train.

Jamilia ran with Isabella and lay under the train. Hashim then went and crawled under as well. Hasani checked his surroundings, then ran out and opened the door. It was a lot heavier than he had expected. But he managed to get it open enough for Jamilia and Hashim to climb in. But when Jamilia stood up, he heard the horses again. This time he saw something worse than his nightmares. His old Master Jon coming with a four of his men and five dogs. They were running right at him. Just then the train started to move. Hasani lifted Isabella onto the train Hashim climbed up and pulled Jamilia into the car. Hasani looked at her just before the train drove off. But he knew that he couldn't put her in danger. He loved her too much. So, he slammed the door and ran away from the train. Jon steered his horse towards him and told two of his men to follow the train. Jon then pulled out his revolver and shot at Hasani, putting him into the ground.

Meanwhile Jamilia and Hashim had trouble of their own. Jon's other men had ridden their horses close to the train and dismounted onto the now moving train. They were able to climb up and make their way to Jamilia on the roofs of the boxcars. Jamilia stood there with Hashim still in shock and disturbed at what had happened to Hasani. She had heard a gunshot but had her hopes up that he would be ok.

Suddenly the roof opened, and two men looked down. Jamilia moved towards the wall. The men dropped through, landing in front of her. Hashim ran over and threw punches at the man. He was able to overpower one of the men. This gave Jamilia the chance she wanted. She ran over to the door and with all her strength opened it up. Looking out she saw that she was on a large bridge. Jumping was not an option so, she formulated a backup plan. She grabbed one of the men by the arm and rolled him out of the train. He went tumbling out, then got stuck under a wheel. The wheel crushed his legs which sent him falling off the bridge.

Jamilia turned and tried to shake the sound of crushing bones from her head. She then and saw the other man stagger onto his feet. The man looked at Jamilia with anger. Then looking at where she was, he laughed. Jamilia was standing in front of the open door. Hashim, out of nowhere, ran up behind him and threw him out of the train right next to Jamilia but the man was holding onto Hashim. The weight of the man, made Hashim slip and there on the middle of the bridge, he hung on for dear life by the door. Jamilia ran up and tried to pull him in. Hashim tried and tried to climb up but knew it was no use and his hands couldn't hold him much longer. He looked up at Jamilia and said, "Get to freedom, don't stop! Do it for Hasani and do it for me." Jamilia, through the tears, told him to keep holding on and she tried to pull him up, but Hashim smiled and said, "Go and be free."

Jamilia watched as he fell from the train over the bridge as if in slow motion. She cried and, in her heart, she promised that every ounce of her living in freedom would be for Hashim. Which reminded her of Hasani, she stood up and looked back hoping to see Hasani, but saw nothing. She was now headed to the place she wanted without the love of her life. To her knowledge he had been shot and killed. But she had to keep hope alive that he was still living.

***

Hasani opened his eyes seeing that someone was dragging him on the ground. His hands were tied together, and the rope was tied to Jon's saddle. Hasani was being drug across the ground. He knew that he would be brutally tortured when they arrived back at the slave plantation. Hasani moved his arms to try to get free but felt excruciating pain in his back. He then realized he had been shot in the back. This would slow him down a lot if he managed to escape. Hasani knew he wouldn't be able to escape, and if he did nobody would be there to treat his wounds. He yelled out to the person who was his only hope. "Jon, I need you to get me out of here. You need to know that it is wrong to keep us as slaves and to torture us. We are people too so please treat us like that." Jon turned around and stopped his horse.

He climbed down and crouched low and looking into Hasani's eyes said, "Hasani, I have actually been thinking about this and I do think that you are right. I realized what I am doing is wrong." He said calmly.

Hasani looked up at him and said, "Are you serious? Thank you. You can be a kind man when needed." Jon walked over to him and pulled out his knife. He put the knife to the rope so he could cut it. But instead, he sliced Hasani's hand. This started to bleed almost immediately. And it hurt even more since the rope was so tight.

Jon just laughed and cruelly said, "Why would you ever think that I would be that kind? I actually didn't lie to you. I do realize what I am doing is wrong, but I don't care at all. I wish my father was dead, my family is gone and my one and only goal in life was to torture you. There is nothing left for me except to make your death long and painful." With that Jon stepped onto Hasani's back making the bullet wound even worse. This sent more pain than Hasani had ever felt in his life. Hasani screamed out in pain, but nobody heard him. Hasani then realized he had to give up on life. He knew that he would never survive.

16 Holding Hope

Meanwhile, on the boxcar, Jamilia began to think about her arrival. Jamilia remembered the reverend giving the instructions of getting off the train before the border or she would die as well. As she planned it out, she thought, "So what if I die. Nobody will care. My sister is probably dead, and I have nobody who even cares about me that would mourn my death." She decided that she would stay on and die if she was found. But as she thought of Hasani she knew that if he were alive then he would want her to keep going. He wouldn't want her to just give up on life. She also knew that if Isabella was left, then her dog would just get another owner who wouldn't treat her as nice as she would. Jamilia stood up and walked towards the open car door. She looked ahead and saw nothing, but knew when the train put on the brakes to slow down, it would be time to get off. It had been forty-five minutes when she felt the train slow down. The train was going around a corner, but she still knew it was going slow.

She grabbed Isabella and waited for the right moment, then leapt from the train. She was lucky that there was a field right there. She fell and let go of Isabella. They both rolled for a little way but were not harmed too much. A few bumps and bruises but no serious injuries.

Jamilia stood up and carried Isabella with her. In front of them was a very large hill. The hill was so big it would take all day to get over. The hill seemed like it could be the border, so she walked towards it with confidence in her heart.

***

Hasani had now arrived back at the slave plantation. Some of the slaves saw him and were scared of what would happen. Jon called all of the slaves to come, and they all met outside the house. Then Jon's father arrived on the porch saying, "Jon, you are not in charge here. You have no authority to kill this man in front of the other slaves. We must keep him. He works hard for…" But before he could finish Jon had taken out his revolver and shot his father in the chest.

"Now that he is dead, I am in charge here. Who would like to go next?" No one spoke. Everyone was too much in shock. "That's what I thought. Now most of my men have died due to this slave. This slave now will slowly die and all of you will watch and see the punishments for escaping from me."

Jon took out his whip and said,
"Everyone line up and whip this man with all of
your strength. If you do not whip him hard
enough you will join him and get whipped as
well." Jon gave the whip to the first man, and he
whipped Hasani very hard. Everyone had their
turn in whipping him. He was almost dead when
they had finished. Hasani didn't care to count
the whippings. When they had finished, the
wounds dried up and hardened. But Jon wasn't
done yet. It was now evening, and Jon was
getting tired, so he stretched out Hasani's arms
making him scream in pain. He tied him up, and
left him at the post for the night. He had two of
his men watch over Hasani all night with loaded
guns and backup swords and knives.

Meanwhile in the slave house there were
three other slaves who were very angry with
what Jon was doing. They had been at the
plantation about as long as Hasani and were done

with his constant turmoil that he inflicted. Matthew, Joseph and Logan all feeling this anger went to every slave and told them their plan. The other slaves were not only willing to help Hasani onto a train, but also risk their own lives in the act. Hasani was too sore and in pain to escape alone but he had tried so hard, and he didn't deserve to be tortured. So, they planned the attack and waited for the right time to free Hasani and possibly themselves. They had to keep in mind that they were risking their lives for another man's freedom.

***

Jamilia and Isabella had climbed this hill all day and night. They had only stopped at the top for a one-hour rest. It had been hard to climb the hill without Hasani by her side. But Isabella was keeping her going. Isabella seemed like she would never rest but at the top she fell asleep in seconds.

They were now almost to the bottom. From the top she could see a forest and a large clearing beyond the forest. But she couldn't see what was in the clearing. Jamilia trucked on hoping to get to Indiana in the next few days. But going those last couple days with little sleep and no food she began to fade. She kept going all the while because she would get there soon and have much food.

After several hours of walking, she finally saw a small house in the distance. It was a small, quaint log cabin. Outside in the back, was a barn with two horses and a wagon. There was a cow, a few pigs, and about a dozen chickens. Seeing all the animals and knowing the food they produced she had to go and ask for rest and something to eat. She walked up to the door and knocked quietly. Nobody came to the door right away. But she did hear a man ask, "Who is there and what do you want?"

Jamilia spoke up and said, "I have been hiking all day with my dog and I need food and sleep." The door was immediately opened but the man and the woman in the house had handkerchiefs over their eyes. Jamilia stepped in and said, "Why do you have your handkerchief over your eyes? Can you not, see?"

But the man said, "We can see just fine, but we will not lie so if we never see you then we don't need to lie to the constable about not seeing you. Now please, we have food and a bed for you to stay in for as long as you want. My name is Aaron Schrock, and this is my wife, Caroline." Jamilia went and ate up dinner and went to bed. She was so thankful that she had stumbled across this honest and honorable Amish family.

***

Hasani had been hanging all night and was very sore. But he was able to now stand instead of hang. He had the strength to hold himself up but not to fight or to run so he didn't even think of escaping. He knew that there would be no chance. He would get caught in seconds and had no help.

***

The night before three of the slaves had planned a way of escape to get Hasani to freedom. They hitched up the horses to the buggy quietly. They were able to get into the house with the help of Sarah. She let them in and gave them kitchen knives and guns that were in the main room. Jon had a gun stand where he kept all of his guns. Sarah was able to get all of the guns off the shelf and give them to the slaves. Since she was a slave who worked in the house,

216

she heard more conversations. Conversations like where they put the keys to the gun shelf.

Their plan was set to happen they just had to have the courage. They both aimed their guns at the guards who were guarding Hasani. With such perfect shots, as if it were a miracle, they shot down the three guards. This woke everyone in the house which then started the third slave Logan's job. He ran over to Hasani and cut the ropes tied to his hands. He was a bigger stronger slave, so he untied Hasani and slumped him over his shoulders. He ran to the buggy which was hitched and ready to go. Hasani was placed across the back seat to lay down. Jon was now out of the house with his revolver in hand. The slaves were surprised at how he had another gun. They realized he must have slept with it. Jon came out firing at every slave in sight. He shot down many slaves who had nothing to do with but had heard the shots. When Jon saw the buggy and the three slaves loading up Hasani, Jon called for an already saddled horse and rode towards them. The slaves had enough time to load Hasani, get onto the buggy and ride away. Jon slapped his horse with the reins and rode after the buggy. Seeing this the slaves also slapped the reigns and yelled for the horses to go faster. Logan grabbed the shotgun seizing the opportunity and shot at Jon. Not having a good position, he missed but continued to fire. Jon, seeing this, lifted his revolver and shot Logan with one shot. Logan fell out of the buggy and landed headlong into a ditch. Logan rolled his head over and said, "Dear God, they deserve to live. Please keep them safe."

The buggy reached the train station. They still had a way to go, and they were happy to see that there was a train there. Their prayers had been answered.

Suddenly, a bullet whizzed by the drivers' head. Jon was right next to the buggy trying to slow them down. The driver yelled back for Logan to shoot him but hearing no response he turned to see Logan was gone. The driver turned to see a revolver in his face. He was quick so he hit the hand holding the gun which sent his arm in the other direction. Jon slowed only for a second but regained his speed and caught up. Jon, seeing Hasani unconscious in the back, contemplated shooting him, but he then knew he could miss, so he sped up his horse and aimed his revolver at the two horses driving the buggy. He had a couple shots left and his gun was only a few feet away from the horse and he was right next to the buggy. He pulled the trigger which was pointed right at the heart of the lead horse.

17 Finally Free

Jamilia had eaten and rested for long enough. It was now time to move. She walked out of the room to see the Amish couple sitting drinking coffee. They both still had their handkerchief over their face. Jamilia said, "Thank you for everything, but I must be on my way."

Mr. Schrock said, "We will always try to do what is right. Be safe out there. You must swim across the river one mile from the bridge. The river is two miles away and when you cross the river you will be a free woman." Jamilia thanked them again, whistled to Isabella and left the house.

They hiked for about a half an hour. She wanted to preserve her energy for the swim. It wouldn't be too hard, but she knew it would be very cold. As she hiked, she thought about lots of things. She thought about Hasani and how he was doing, she prayed that he had survived the gunshot and was on his way to freedom. She also knew that Hashim had died with his whole heart serving the Lord Jesus, he was now rejoicing with the Lord in heaven. Another thing that came to mind was her family. She knew nothing about where her family was, but she knew that they were taken away as slaves and so she had no idea if she would ever see them again.

She hiked the two miles then turned. Seeing the bridge, she walked the other way. In about fifteen minutes she arrived at a trail that had been manmade. She walked down with Isabella and stepped into the water. It was very cold, but she couldn't think about that now. She was so close to freedom. She jumped in and began swimming, not thinking about the cold. Isabella was right in front of her swimming fast. They both made it across in a good time, but the cold was making Jamilia not think straight. She cried out for help and wasn't able to yell loud enough. Without being able to think straight she didn't feel motivated to climb up the small hill to her new home. Isabella climbed into her arms and Jamilia hugged her very tight. Jamilia then fell asleep there at the side of an ice-cold river.

***

He had the gun only a few feet from the horse's side. This was a clear fire shot which would also flip the buggy and send it into the ditch. Jon shot but all they heard was a click. Jon had thought he had loaded his gun but it was clear he had no more bullets. It was a miracle. Seizing the opportunity, the slave steered the

buggy into Jon. Jon was trying to get his horse
out of the way. But he was not able to since he
was now right at the edge of the road. So, he
pulled the horse faster to get out of the way. But
the driver reached out and grabbed him by the
shirt. The driver pulled him backwards with all
his strength. This sent Jon falling off the back of
his horse and into the ditch. With that they were
able to speed away and catch up to the train that
was just closing its doors.

When they got there the two slaves who
had helped Hasani got out and picked up Hasani
and were able to get onto the caboose before it
picked up too much speed. When they got on,
they were glad to see that they were the only
ones on the caboose. They laid Hasani across the
chairs on one side for him to rest. He had
already been through so much pain that he just
needed to rest. But before he fell asleep, he

thought about Jamilia and how he would be with his wife soon enough and they would be free.

**

Jamilia awoke the next day in another unfamiliar room. There, at her feet, was Isabella curled up asleep. It puzzled Jamilia because the last thing she remembered was she was by the river freezing almost to death. She then heard conversation between two women. One of the voices was vaguely familiar but she couldn't place it. The other voice she had never heard in her life. One woman walked into the room. She was a white woman with bright red hair. Jamilia thought that they were going to kill her or torture her. But when the woman saw that Jamilia was awake her face brightened into a giant smile. She then turned and yelled through the curtain, "Tiana, your sister is awake!" Jamilia couldn't believe it. Her eyes immediately filled with tears

225

as her big sister ran into the room with tears in her own eyes. Tiana embraced her baby sister who she had not seen in years. They hugged each other so much that they didn't want to let go. They had a lot of catching up to do.

Later that day, Jamilia was fitted into new clothes. The clothes were like nothing that she had ever seen before. The only other nice dress she had ever worn was the dress that she wore in her wedding. Jamilia was given a leash for Isabella. Her sister came back in later and told her they were going to the shops. Jamilia was surprised that they were just able to walk through different shops and be able to buy things. Jamilia looked at all the white and black people around and she didn't see any hate. There was an older white man sitting and talking with an older black man. They seemed happy as well. There were some white shop owners selling food to black people. And there was a black mother with her three kids buying fabrics. There were no slaves there were only people. Jamilia looked at the white people with little fear, but they looked back at her like she was just a human and no different. Jamilia liked this.

Jamilia and her sister walked through most of the shops getting things. It was so good to finally be able to walk with no fear of people chasing. After shopping for a while, they went back to Tiana's house. The house was right on the outskirts of Fairmount, Indiana. Her property was about ten acres. There was a large house and there was a barn with two horses, one cow, one goat and sixteen chickens. Tiana had gotten all this for working hard in Indiana. She was working at a bakery in town making and selling bread. She was working to pay for her sister's freedom and her father, but she had never known where they had gone. She had worked for this big house so that she could once again live with her sister and her father.

18 Kentucky

Hasani awoke with a start. Something had happened. He had slept for hours on end. He knew he had overslept and had to get moving. There was still pain in his back but it was just a little sore, but he would be able to walk alone. He knew that he had only healed this much by the power of God. Hasani saw that his other three companions had disappeared, but that was most likely because they saw their chance to get to freedom. They knew Hasani would just slow them down. He climbed out of the stopped train and was surprised to see that the rest of the train was gone all that was left was the caboose; n the caboose was one canteen of water and a six-inch dagger. His companions must have found it and left it for him. The caboose was in the middle of a dense forest. Hasani walked around to scope out the area.

Again, Hasani had the feeling again that someone was watching him. He looked around and tried to be as quiet as he could. His hand tightly gripped his knife he had found in the train and waited until he found what he knew had to be around. Seeing nothing, he went back into the caboose. There on the seat was a box the others must have left for him. There inside the box was a wrap for injuries, three cans of food, two cans of beans and one can of apples. He opened up the apples right away and gobbled them down. He then grabbed the bean can and the cover caught his eye. It said, "Isabella's Cold Beans." This reminded him of Isabella. Isabella was so nice to him. She even risked her life for his. Just seeing that it was the same brand of beans made him cry. He cried because Isabella reminded him of his wife. He had no idea how she was doing. He had no idea if she was still alive for that matter. Glancing outside he saw something shiny in the grass, but thinking it was just the tracks ignored it. After he had eaten all of the beans, he went out to get it because he had nothing to lose. The second he stepped out of the caboose a shovel hit him in the head and knocked him out cold.

Hasani awoke hours later with an older black man's head looking over him. Hasani sat up and asked, "Where am I and who are you?"

The man said, "My name is Solomon Nelson, and you are at a plantation in Kentucky. You were dropped off last night by my master Judah Smith."

Hasani was confused, but the man continued, "We need to go out to work. If you do not come, our master kills his slaves. He is not mean enough to torture us, but he will just kill to end it. So please come and work and don't make this hard for us.

Hasani stood up and said with a sigh, "Ok, what do I need?" Hasani hated it, but he was at another slave plantation, and he didn't know the way if he even tried to escape.

Four months later, in December 1865, he was still at this place. He had lost all hope of ever escaping and seeing Jamilia again. He knew there was no way that she could possibly be alive still. It was hard for him to deal with at first but over time he was able to figure out his new life. He had gotten to know Mr. Nelson very well. They both had talked for hours about almost everything that there was to talk about. He said that he was taken into slavery and hadn't seen his two daughters in years. His wife was killed in front of him before he was taken. But the man had always kept his daughters in his heart.

Mr. Nelson told Hasani about how if he had a chance to leave, he would go to Indiana and look for his girls until he died. Hasani told him about his wife and their dog. He had left them on the train and had no clue to if she was alive or dead. But he had given up hope. Mr. Nelson told him to never give up hope. But it was too hard for Hasani to think about her without weeping.

That day they were getting things ready for their master's Christmas. They were doing things like cleaning the yard for guests and making sure the house was looking nice and even helping decorate. They had heard rumors from the overseers that something was going on in the United States government. The master had been talking about it late into the night. He seemed furious. Hasani and Mr. Nelson didn't know what it was, but it was bad for their master. Today especially they were saying that "it" was going to happen in eight days. They also heard that they would just send them and make them do the working. Hasani thought it was about them, but he wasn't sure.

As Hasani was shoveling snow his master walked out. The master was already having a very bad day. That morning he had gotten mad that one of his slaves didn't bring him his breakfast right away. But Hasani had his back to him. Suddenly Hasani threw the snow and it crashed all over master Judah's head. Hasani had no idea that he was there. Judah's face was much redder now. Hasani knew he was going to get killed. He was right. Judah pulled out his revolver and pointed it at Hasani. But then he put it down and said, "I can't shoot you. You are one of my best men and I need your work for the last eight days."

Hasani thought about what Judah had said all day and into the night. What did he mean by, "The last eight days?" Were they going to be set free or would they all be killed? Hasani had so many questions but no answers.

Over the course of the next few days things started changing. Judah wasn't out yelling at them like he used to. And all the slaves had more free time. Finally, on December 6, 1865, Judah called all of the slaves to the house. He announced what he needed to right away. "The president of the United States, Abraham Lincoln, just issued a new law that slavery has been abolished in the United States."

After he said this all the slaves erupted in cheering and excitement. Hasani was too shocked to even respond. He didn't think anything like this would ever happen in America. Judah spoke up again and took out a folded piece of paper saying, "Here is a map of the United States. This should get you on your way. The X is where we are." With that he stomped inside grumbling. Hasani grabbed the map and held it up for everyone to see. Hasani also got a look and was able to see that they just had to go north, and they would run into Indiana. He dropped the map and ran to find Mr. Nelson.

When he heard the news, Mr. Nelson thanked God and asked, "So, if we are going to Indiana, we had better get a move on." He had been sleeping and hadn't heard the announcement. They packed up and headed to Indiana to start a new life. Hasani knew that he was finally free. He had gotten to become free while alive; although he would forever have scars on his back, but he was alive. All of the slaves went to the train station. Some got tickets for the train from the money they had saved. Others were able to start a life with their family there. Hasani and Mr. Nelson got a train ticket for Indiana. They were finally going to be in Indiana.

19 Reunited

Hasani and Mr. Nelson arrived on Christmas Eve. There had been many stops and they had to catch another train. It was snowing when they got there. They ran to every inn trying to find somewhere warm to stay, but to no avail. The inns were already full and didn't want to take them in even if they had room. But one owner gave them both blankets. These blankets froze around them covering their full body. Although they both loved being free this wasn't what they had in mind.

They stumbled around the town all afternoon. Finally, around midnight, just as they were about to give up hope, two young women saw them and said, "Men, please come to our house and get warm. We have enough rooms to fit you in. Please come and warm up for the night." Hasani was too cold to look up and thank her. They both were too cold that their brains weren't working right. They weren't even able to walk straight. But the girls helped at their best. When they reached the house, they were led up the stairs to a room that was fixed nicely. The house was very warm, and they were left in the room to warm up and rest. When their blankets had thawed, they took them off and got into a warm bed. Within seconds they had fallen asleep.

The next day Hasani woke up to a rooster crowing. Looking around, he saw Mr. Nelson sleeping next to him. He gently woke him and said, "We were given a place to sleep last night. I don't remember that happening, do you? They both got out of the bed and quietly went to the door. Hasani opened it and saw that they were at the top of a staircase. They both heard two voices talking. They walked down the steps quietly and stepped into a dining room. There sitting at the table were Jamilia and Tiana. Hasani yelled out, "Jamilia!" Jamilia looked up and dropped her bowl, breaking it on the ground.

Mr. Nelson, who was still behind the wall, looked at him confused and walked out to see. Seeing the girls, he ran to them weeping. When the girls saw Mr. Nelson, they both began crying and hugging him as tightly as they could. Mr. Nelson was their father! When they had reunited with their father, Hasani walked over and Jamilia caught him and embraced him crying even more. Hasani was so confused, and he had so many questions. But he had Jamilia, so the thought left his mind. Hasani hugged her back and he cried too. They then embraced in a passionate kiss.

Mr. Nelson stood up and squeezed Hasani's arm and said, "Hasani what are you doing? This is my daughter. How dare you?"

Hasani looked over at him and was about to speak, but was cut off by Jamilia, who said, "Pa, this is Hasani. He is my husband, and he risked his life to save me."

Mr. Nelson said, "Why did you never tell me this before? If you had told me your wife's name, we would have known each other much better.

Tiana stepped in and said, "We are all back together. Let's go into the sitting room and catch up with each other." Tiana held her Pa's hand and headed that way.

Jamilia said, "Tiana, we will meet you in there soon I want to talk to Hasani about something."

Tiana smiled and said, "Don't get carried away you lovebirds."

Hasani kissed Jamilia again and said, "Jamilia you don't even know how much I missed you."

Jamilia said, "When you put me on the train, what happened? I heard a gunshot. Were you shot by Jon? What happened after that? How did you meet my father?"

Hasani put up his hands in self-defense, "Woah there, that was four questions. How about I will answer one question if you answer one for me."

Jamilia blushed and said, "What happened when you put me on the train?"

Hasani sighed and said, "I was shot in the back by Jon. He then took me back to our old home. From there I was helped out by other slaves. We got on the train and only got to Kentucky. I was then taken captive and brought into slavery where your father was. When slavery was abolished, we were able to come here. Now my turn. I want to know what happened to you and how you survived."

Jamilia looked up and said, "Well, I did what you said and stay on the train. But I remembered what the reverend said, and I got off early. I was able to stay at a nice family's house. From there I came to a river and when I swam across, I fell unconscious. But my sister found me and here I am. Oh, I love you, Hasani, and I missed you so much."

They embraced in another kiss, but they were interrupted by Tiana who said, "Hey, you two you both coming we are waiting for you? You can't just stand there kissing forever." Hasani laughed and headed into the room. He was so happy he had finally been with Jamilia again. He was living every one of his greatest dreams.

20 Change in the Heart and Mind

It had been two years since Hasani had been reunited with Jamilia, her sister and their father. Hasani was now a father. Hasani and Jamilia had a baby boy on October 19, 1866. They named their son Daniel after the meaning: God is my Judge. Hasani had grown closer to Christ. He had even become the pastor of a church in Indiana. He was the pastor of a mixed-race church. Since Abraham Lincoln, the President of the united states had made slavery illegal now people began to change. Many white men now began to except black people. It took time but things were starting to change.

One Sunday he was getting ready for another service that he would bring to the congregation. He had planned this message all week and was excited to share it with his congregation. His topic was on forgiveness and how God can give it to everyone. Hasani put on his black suit and tie. Hasani was nervous, he had preached every Sunday since he became pastor but today was different. The sermon he had prepared was covering forgiving people who were hard to forgive. He tightened his tie and Jamilia walked in and folded down his collar. She then turned him and put her arms around his neck. She looked him in the eyes and said, "You will do well today. There is no need to be nervous. We can go and spend the day at the lake after if you want. We could have a picnic with us two and Daniel."

Daniel ran into the room and jumped into Hasani who caught him and threw him in the air and swung him over his shoulders. Daniel laughed and gripped onto Hasani's hair. Hasani walked out to the living room and sat down at the table, greeting Isabella who ran to him for a good scratch. Hasani rubbed her right where she liked it, then gave her some leftover meat from the night before. He then pulled down Daniel and gave him to his mother. There was some new hot bread and butter that they had for breakfast with cold milk. The church was only a short way, but he lifted his wife and Daniel into the wagon. He then climbed up and grabbed the reigns to his horse and headed to church. The morning was beautiful, and the birds were singing. It was a perfect day to have a picnic and go to church.

Once they arrived at the church, they greeted people as they came in and gave out hymn books. When the singing had begun Hasani, and everyone stood up and sang the songs that had been chosen. Concluding the singing, he walked up to the podium. Placing his Bible down he looked out over the congregation, and began, "The topic I have chosen today has been hard for me to prepare. I was a slave like some of you before slavery was abolished. It has been hard to forgive those who have treated us so terribly. But we need to remember God was able to forgive everyone and die for our sins so we need to be able to pass on that forgiveness to others even if it might be difficult."

When Hasani finished his message, he prayed over the congregation that they would be able to forgive their neighbors. He then dismissed the church and people began to leave. Hasani stepped down from the stage and walked over to Jamilia and Daniel. He put his arm around Jamilia, and they left. Jamilia said, "I told you that you would do good." Hasani thanked her and got into the wagon.

Jamilia had packed a picnic lunch and they went to the lake to spend the afternoon. When they arrived, they laid down the blanket and Jamilia set out the food. Hasani picked up Daniel and walked down to the water, where he saw a man sitting on the beach. Hasani being the friendly man that he was, introduced himself. The man turned and looked at Hasani. When they made eye contact, they were both shocked at who they saw. Hasani set down Daniel and gave the man a big hug. They both were crying and laughing at the same time. They hadn't seen each other in so long.

Hasani invited him to have lunch with them and the man said that he would. They walked over to Jamilia who saw them with a puzzled look on her face. Hasani said, "Jamilia, I know you don't recognize him, but I would like to re-introduce you to my brother Kamau.

Jamilia stood up and gave him a hug saying, "It is so good to see you again. I am so thankful that we found you. Kamau sat down and they had lunch together.

Later that day as they had finished lunch they were walking to the wagon, when they saw another man. It was the face of the man they hoped they would never see again. When the man saw them, he walked over. Hasani saw him and quickly put his head down. When Kamau saw him, he threw a punch to the stranger knocking him to the ground. The man fell to the ground and did not defend himself. He took out his gun and turned it to give it to Kamau. Kamau spit on the man then took the gun. He aimed the gun at their evil old master Jon Hundley. He laughed at the man and said, "I hate you, but I know how you treated Hasani so I will let him kill you." Kamau handed the gun to Hasani.

Hasani with a trembling hand he pointed it at Jon's face. But he couldn't pull the trigger.

Jon said, "Remember how I whipped you, I shot you and I was evil to you, now kill me! I deserve it!" Jamilia was crying now. Hasani tensed his arm and pointed the gun at him and was about to pull the trigger.

But through the anger Hasani felt God saying to him, "I forgave you; can you not forgive another man?" Hasani remembered the sermon he had given that day. The sermon had been about forgiving people who were hard to forgive.

Hasani lowered the gun and said, "I can't kill you. I am a Christian and Jesus forgave me by dying for me. I want to be like my Lord so I will not kill you. Jon thanked him and walked away with his head in his hands crying. Even if he never would become a Christian Hasani felt better for forgiving the man who had made his life miserable.

Kamau looked at Hasani and said, "Why did you not kill him? You had a chance to kill the man who made you go through hell. Why wouldn't you? Nobody would have judged you for it."

Hasani looked at his brother and said, "God would have judged me. I will not kill him because Jesus didn't kill me when I didn't follow him."

Kamau said, "You are right Hasani. I have not been the best Christian lately. I want to be like you. You are the man who all boys should grow up to be like.

Hasani looked at his brother and put his hand on his shoulder and said, "It's all God. I learned this from God, dear brother."

--.--

"And that is how I want my kids and grandkids to grow up to be. So how did you like the story? I thought you would like something with action and adventure. I wanted to tell you a story that would be like all the blockbuster movies that you like. So, what did you all learn?" Asked Grandpa.

Chandler was the first to speak, "I learned how to treat women. Women are to be treated with respect and honor."

Charlie said, "I learned that real stories are better than Instagram stories and stuff online. I want to read more books from history."

Charlette thought about it for a second and said, "I learned that all people are created equal. We are all people created by God. So, we should treat everyone we meet with respect and honor. The color of their skin shouldn't matter but it should be just like if we were making friends with other people of our color. I am so thankful that today you came Grandpa. Please come by and visit again."

Chandler and Charlie both agreed with their sister and asked, "When you come next time can you tell us another story?"

Grandpa nodded and said, "Well, I hope you enjoyed that story. Now, I got to get home for dinner with your grandma." The three kids all waved goodbye, pocketed their phones, and went upstairs.

When their mom got home, she saw that her dad was gone. She went upstairs to get the kids for dinner. She expected them to be in their room on their phones. But when she opened the door, she was shocked to see that they were not there. She walked downstairs and looked out the back window. There in the back yard were her three kids who used to be addicted to their phones throwing a football. They never threw the football around. She called them all in and they raced in to have dinner. When they got to the door a police car pulled up. Seeing it was their dad, they ran down and gave him a big hug. Dad who was shocked by their surprise hugged them back. They finally walked inside to have dinner with his family. They all sat down and ate the Pizza that mom had bought. Before they ate all three of the kids took their turns and prayed for the dinner. Mom was so surprised by what had changed, but she was thankful. She was happy to spend the time she had with the people she loved most.

GRACIE HEIDER

GUARDIAN
ANGELS

Those
who can
must...

Guardian Angels - Gracie Heider

Chapter 1: Longshots and flirts

Hetz's leg shook uncontrollably, he had long ago given up the attempts to check it. Forcing himself to take another breath, he stroked Jack's hand with his thumb. Gratefully she squeezed it back, though even that slight motion sent her joints aching again. And there they sat for the next three hours as people paraded in front of them looking into the open coffin.

That's the thing you will soon realize about this book- it is not by any means an advertisement for Guardian Angels. After reading this, you may be disgusted with the program as a whole. Sometimes I am. I've seen too much. Too many funerals. But it's Jack and Hetz's story that really gets me because these kids don't deserve this. They deserve to be living the carefree life of a teenager who has just gotten their license. They deserve to be happy. They deserve to feel safe. But if there is one thing that life will teach you, it is this - Safety is in the eye of the beholder.

~~~

Jack Marris and Hetz MacArthur were awkwardly close. They both knew it but neither one of them dared break it off. In fact, when Jack told him to breathe opposite her so that they could both get a full breath she whispered it directly into his ear.

To literally anybody else getting stuck with either Jack or Hetz in this position might have made you remarkably uncomfortable. Both of them somehow managed to be shockingly good looking. And I say somehow because Jack rarely, if ever, tried to look nice on purpose. And Hetz- well he was too handsome for his own good, and was rather fond of the effect he had on the ladies he encountered.

But* (I highlight this because I am well aware of what you are assuming and I have been told to make it abundantly clear. Thus, the bold but) as best friends, they spent very little time dwelling on the appearances of the other unless it was Jack telling Hetz that he was "The ugliest looking critter on God's good earth" whenever his flirting got out of hand. Or when they had completed a particularly challenging workout and Hetz commented on Jack's fairly sweaty, frizzy hair.

That being said, even though they had no romantic feelings for each other the fact was that they were pressed together in the cabinet. Legs and arms were completely entangled and Jack had had the misfortune to get in first. Meaning Hetz was now crammed against her.

"You stink." she wrinkled her nose dramatically. She knew that if he could have moved, he would have given her an extremely distended look, matching her antics.

"Well, that's weird. It's not like I wa-" he broke off as footsteps thundered by them. After a second of respectful silence, he continued. "It's not like I was running through a massive warehouse a minute ago in like four-hundred-degree weather or anything like that." In all honesty it was 100-ish degrees. A far cry from four hundred sure, but once you get that hot and you're sitting in a cabinet with another equally as sweaty person it's all the same. They continued to wait a few more sweltering minutes until finally Jack kicked Hetz out of the cupboard, evidently deeming it safe to do so. When she joined him, she was shocked to find that they weren't as alone as she thought.

People. She thought. *More blooming people than I ever want to see in an active shooter situation.* A quick conformational glance at Hetz sent them both into action. "I'm gonna need you guys to come with me." Hetz said, flashing a winning smile at the group of people and setting off to herd them to safety.

Jack started to sprint in the opposite direction directly toward the now running sound of gunfire.

Oh yes, right I forgot that you have just met Jack. No, she's not deaf, no she's not stupid, - most of the time that is.

She was running toward the shooter on purpose.

But not on a whim of heroism, sure she was the type of person to just jump on a situation like that, but this time she actually knew what she was doing. And it wasn't the first time she had done it.

"Get down!" A twenty something young man said as he caught her eye as she ran by, and when he saw that she wasn't planning on stopping he dove out and together they skidded across the aisle and landed in a mass.

She shoved him off. "What the heck are you doing?"

"Saving your life most likely!" He yelled back, but then he seemed to process just exactly who he had saved.

"Actually, it's more likely that I'm gonna save yours." she said, kicking his leg over about half an inch. Just as a bullet made a hole in the floor where it had rested a moment before.

"How did you kno-"

"I'm a sniper myself." she said casually, like when you realize that someone has the same hobby as you. So, at ease in fact that the boy was fairly blown away,

"You're a- Why the heck are you?" He gave up, he was smart enough to realize he probably wasn't going to get any information out of her. Instead, he went for a different approach, "Then again- I changed my mind. I don't think I mind a pretty thing like you saving my life."

"Good grief. I'm gonna need you to take it way the heck down." She said dramatically, putting her hand way down by the floor. *Gosh I might throw up.* She thought, finally she spotted her two older bracket mates working their way toward her, stopping just across the aisle. There was only a slight obstacle between them. The fact that that aisle was in clear view of the shooter. But for Jack it didn't really matter, choking down a rush of adrenaline she forced her body to go from shaking into a controlled state then, without warning she sprinted across the aisle.

Some say that pain is relative. Usually Jack would disagree, but as she sprinted for the cover of the pile of crates, subsequently slamming her foot into the edge of it as she dove for cover, right then, at that moment, the pain she was feeling was the worst pain in the entire world.

And granted, minus the sliding into a wooden crate, you could most likely sympathize with Jack. The moment you stub your toe, you experience true pain.

But unlike Jack, you are probably not getting shot at. (I assume so, that is. If not - well hats off to you my good friend)

If she had taken a second to think about it, which she rarely did, she would have pulled her body fully into the meager cover that the box offered to avoid the hail of bullets that were aimed at her. Instead, it was up to her two older team mates to bring her into the relative safety of the wooden barricade and their embrace. "Good. Grief." she spit out trying to stifle a scream.

"Are you hit Jack?" Matt asked scanning her for telltale blood.

"If getting hit with a box count." she said cradling her foot in her hand.

Matt flicked her on the forehead. "You have got to be kidding me!"

"It hurts!" she spat back.

"Pull yourself together Marris!" Hawk, her senior bracket member, who never called her by anything but her last name, yelled at her over the chaos of the firefight they were engaged in.

Jack gave one last glance of her throbbing foot before rolling over into a shooting position to provide cover for Hetz to join them.

There was no time to nurse wounds when you worked Jack's job.

Ultimately, the world needed saving and Jack, Hetz and their team, Foxtrot, were some of the few people who were willing to do it, but it hasn't always been that way.

Available now on Amazon go support her work!

Bibliography

Articles

https://www.history.com/topics/black-history/underground-railroad

https://www.nationalgeographic.org/encyclopedia/underground-railroad/

https://www.historynet.com/underground-railroad/

Movies/Documentary's

(Kassie Lemmons) Harriet - 2019

(Peter Cousens) Freedom - 2014

(Paul Wendkos) A Woman Called Moses - 1978

(Orlando Bagwell) Roots of Resistance - 1990

(Steve McQueen) 12 Years a Slave - 2013

Books

Gateway to Freedom - Eric Foner

The Underground Railroad - Colson Whitehead

From Slavery to Freedom - Fredrick Douglass

Up from Slavery - Booker T. Washington

12 Years a Slave - Solomon Northup

Soul by Soul - Walter Johnson

About the Author

Noah is the 3rd born of 7 sons, and 2 daughters and was raised in an environment of adventure and laughter with Christ Jesus as the center. Since birth, he has had a love for words, written and spoken. He was an avid reader and identifies strongly with the characters he reads about.

He wrote his first book around age 10 about "Froggy," and kept his parents on his toes with his vibrant personality and strong will. As a young child, his spoken stories were often a wild tale of his adventures that got bigger and better, every time they were told. He has an imagination filled with untold stories, characters and books that may someday find themselves published.

This book was written when Noah was 16 years old. He has a desire to make you smile, cry, laugh and get lost in the pages and plot of his books. He hopes that you will identify, in some way, with the characters, and understand what they are feeling and experiencing.

Noah loves the Lord and has a desire to serve Him with his life. He loves his family and friends and enjoys meeting new people and visiting new places.

Made in United States
Orlando, FL
02 June 2022